The Burqa Master

Cid Andrenelli

Published by FeedARead.com Publishing – Arts Council funded

A CIP catalogue record for this title is available from the British Library.

For Francesco

Contents

Introduction

The Burqa Master is a novel play; it flows from scene to scene in the same way we would watch a film, yet has the added elements of a novel.

Unlike a traditional play with only dialogue and brief scenes I have fleshed out the story using prose-poetry and narrative relating to the characters. Instead, the dialogues are written in the more dynamic play format and through them revelation and conflict come about.

At the end of the Burqa Master novel I've included the original one act theatre play, which is written for the stage.

I have always loved reading prose-poetry, novels and plays and wished to combine these genres into one work of fiction. This novel play is a fusion of literary forms that I hope you will enjoy.

Cid Andrenelli

CHARACTERS

Old Man (Behdad Babai)
Hamid Babai
Faruzeh Babai
Abbas
Hosro
Jamshid Mohamed
Zina Mohamed
Patty Mcluskey
Pete Pratt
Melanie
Mr Akbar
Mummy Akbar
Fatima Akbar
Hafsa Akbar
Sepideh
Sadam
Selma
Amjad
Koosha
Amina
Carla
Dwarf Doll (Jamshid's mother)
Uncle Aziz
Minor characters include: Selma's two sons, Jamshid's father and son, the women at the factory and the women at the oriental dance classes.

The Burqa Master

Behdad Babai left Iran with his wife, son and daughter in 1979. The family settled down to live in a cheap two bedroom flat in South London. Behdad opened a tiny shop and the children went to the local school. His wife stayed shut up in the flat and tied a washing line round the toilet and hung herself out the window.

Some years later his daughter Faruzeh got pregnant. She dropped out of university and married a bucked-toothed man called Abbas. His son Hamid left school at sixteen and went to work in the family shop.

Hamid also signed up for an acting agency and over the years he's had many roles. He's been a dirt covered Egyptian slave, whipped while pulling boulders across the desert to build pyramids. He's played the part of a guard in a sultan's desert harem, wielding a massive dagger and wearing a pair of baggy pantaloons with a black scarf wound round his head. His favourite role was for a TV advert, as an Arab oil sheik massaging a blonde woman in the hot sand with exotic fruits, while she cried, 'Oh my God!' and ate ice cream.

Twenty years on and the family are still there. Behdad is now an old man and his son Hamid is un-married, he says he never found the right one. Hamid's sister and her husband sometimes wish the old man would drop dead and their son Hosro dreams of girls with big bosoms.

13

BABAI FLAT/DAY

The Babai's flat is on the second floor of a tower block on a busy road full of charity shops.

The flat is ugly with cheap plywood veneered doors and plastic gold door handles. The rooms are decorated in peachy colours and crammed with chandeliers and wall lamps.

OLD MAN'S BEDROOM

Early morning in a grey dawn light the old man Behdad Babai sleeps upon a large high iron bed with brass posts. His son Hamid and Hosro his grandson sleep below him on zed beds. Stuck on the bedroom walls are posters of Arab pop stars, pictures of holy men, and hanging from the curtain rail are coat hangers loaded with clothes. Suddenly the alarm clock rings, it's old fashioned with a harsh bell.

The old man springs up to a sitting position, he has shaggy white hair and a beard, and he's wearing a long stained tunic. He swings his legs out of bed and then reaches for his teeth in a glass on the bedside table. He clears his throat of phlegm and spits in the glass, then puts his teeth in.

Old man: *(Shouts.)* Get out of bed you two!

The old man stands up and wavers unsteadily as though about to fall backwards on to the bed, then he takes several steps forward. He stands between the two zed beds looking at Hamid who is unconscious to the world. He fixes his sight on a large walking stick leaning against the wardrobe. He picks it up and jabs at Hamid's stomach.

Old man: Get out of bed, get and wash it's time for prayers, get up you lazy rotter. *(Burps.)*

Meanwhile Hosro sixteen years old with acne, wakes up bleary eyed and guardedly gets out of bed on the other side hiding his erection. There's hardly any room and he stumbles, squeezing himself out between the bed and the wall. Hamid slaps vainly at the walking stick trying to raise himself up.

Hamid: OK OK, I'm coming, I'M COMING, WILL YOU LAY OFF!

The old man takes a step forwards then backwards, turns and tosses the stick up on his bed and leaves the room. Hamid leans out of bed and grabs his trousers, he pulls out a pack of cigarettes and lights one taking a long drag with his eyes half closed.

His almond eyes look like they've been lined with thick black kohl, and his long curling lashes like they've been brushed with mascara. His full red lips smile and he idly scratches his man breasts and chubby belly.

Then he gets out of bed dressed in his underpants. He goes to the window shoves it open and sticks his head outside. Leaning out of the window, still smoking he watches the dawn creeping around the block of flats.

CORRIDOR/BATHROOM

The wide corridor is cluttered with shoes and bicycles and the door to the bathroom is open. The old man is sitting on the toilet seat washing his feet in the bidet. His toenails are long, thick and yellowed with black grime stuck underneath.

Hosro is standing at the washbasin splashing water furiously over his face and hair. He straightens up and runs his fingers backwards spiking up his hair into a crest, then he hastily flattens it back down.

Hamid arrives at the door with a bundle of clothes under his arm. He stares into the bathroom, turns away and pads bare foot into the kitchen.

KITCHEN

Hamid turns on the kitchen sink taps leaving the water running, then he goes to the fridge and takes out a pint of milk. He shoves the cold glass bottle neck in his mouth and lets the milk pour straight into his guts. He turns to the stove, unscrews a moka coffee machine and smashes the filter on the side of the sink to empty the coffee dregs. The old man appears in the doorway.

Old man: Coffee later, it's time to pray….

Hamid looks at him, drops the rest of the moka in the sink and sticks his head under the water flow. The old man goes to the fridge and rummages inside.

Old man: Where's my insulin?

The old man sits on a kitchen chair holding a syringe; he pulls up his skirt and gives his thigh a jab. Hamid dries his head with a towel. The old man chucks his syringe at the sink then grasps the edge of the table and hauls himself to his feet, holding on to the kitchen units he stumbles to the door like a drunkard, a blind man, swinging through the doorframe like an old chimpanzee.

SITTING ROOM

The sitting room looks like a junk shop, overloaded with brass trinkets and cheap oriental souvenirs everywhere. The dining table has a vase filled with plastic flowers and wall units are full to bursting with dinner sets and glassware. The sofa has been pushed back to accommodate three prayer rugs all facing Mecca, one of the rugs has an incorporated compass. There's a large portable stereo cassette player that's blasting a muezzin chant calling them to prayers.

The old man, Hamid and Hosro are praying. After a few bows and prostrations, Hamid still in his underpants gets up from his carpet and leaves the room. The other two don't notice and carry on praying.

BATHROOM

Hamid is back in the bathroom standing with a fluffy white bath towel wrapped round his waist. The room is steamy and he reaches up and wipes away the condensation from the mirror. There's loud muezzin chanting in the background.

He rummages in his sister's makeup bag and chooses a small jar of wrinkle cream that he applies under his eyes. He smiles to himself in the mirror while slapping himself quickly under his chin and then he sprays himself with deodorant.

He sits down on the toilet lid while he cleans his teeth, next to him is a toilet roll holder made from a doll in a long frilly flamenco dress. Her legs are stuck through the tube and her skirt is pulled over the paper roll; her long black hair is held by a pink rose comb and covered by a black net mantilla. Her breasts are hard and pointed and she grips a pair of castanets in one hand and a fancy black lace fan in the other. Her eyes as black as coal keep watch, and her shiny lips as red as cherries always smile, while the family use the toilet, lifting her skirt up and down a dozen times a day.

KITCHEN

Hamid wrapped in his towel is spreading jam on buttered toast and the moka is bubbling on the stove.

There's still loud muezzin chanting in the background.

SITTING ROOM

Hamid is sitting at the table having breakfast, he's dreamily and dispassionately watching his father praying while Hosro is no longer there. The cassette player clicks off abruptly in mid cry and the old man is suspended in mid undulation. He crawls across the carpet on his hands and knees and pulls himself to his feet by grabbing hold of the shelving unit. He picks up the huge cassette player and starts shaking it, and then he bangs it down and pulls out the tape that has unravelled.

17

Old man: *(Looking at Hamid.)* Finished already? Stuffing
    your face! Where's Hosro?

Hamid: Gone back to bed if he's got any sense.

Old man: Any sense? Like his parents still in bed
    sleeping, it's a shame!

The old man leaves the room; he starts banging on their
bedroom door. His daughter Faruzeh and Abbas his son-
in-law are still sleeping or ignoring him. Hamid pours a
second cup of coffee.

Old man: Get up you lazy pigs! *(Loud knocking.)* Too lazy
    to pray! *(Loud thud and crack.)* Too lazy to give your
    son his breakfast!

Hamid: *(Calling into the corridor from the table.)* DAD! It's
    only half past five. *(More banging on door.)* DAD!
    (Hamid starts to stand.) DAD!

STREET OUTSIDE BABAI FLAT/DAY

(Later that morning.) Hamid is sitting astride his scooter
outside the block of flats on the front courtyard. With his
helmet on and a large black satchel across his shoulder
he's ready to go. He zips up his leather jacket and puts on
a pair of small round black sunglasses.

Next to him the old man is standing like a dried up tree in
his white tunic, which billows in the early breeze against
his stick legs. Over his tunic he's wearing a black suit
jacket, fez hat, dark socks and sandals. While Hamid and
his father talk a man leaves the building; the man keeps
his head down ignoring them.

Old man: Ask that thicko thicko Salim for fifty boxes to
    tide us over, your sister will be along after lunch and
    Abbas is waiting here until you let him know about
    the shipment. *(To the man who's walking past.)* Good
    morning. *(To his back.)* A FINE MORNING…. *(Turns
    back to Hamid.)* If it's arrived he'll pick it up on his
    rounds.

Hamid: Yeah Dad, OK, I gotta go….

18

Old man: Wait! Bring home a tin of Okho Chi and some boxes of Gaz. I want the ones that have the picture of the owner on the lid. *(Hamid starts up his scooter and drives out onto the road.)*

The old man is left alone. He turns and slowly walks back into the block of flats.

Hamid drives along the busy street. He weaves through the traffic coming to a halt at the lights. He checks the drivers to his left and right through the mirror, he checks his teeth too and smoothes his eyebrows while revving his scooter. Then left through the winding market streets, driving around the stalls to the family shop. He pulls up outside and turns off the engine.

OUTSIDE SHOP/DAY

Hamid un-padlocks the iron shutters and pulls them halfway open. He stoops to pick up a large pile of Arab and Asian newspapers tied with string and ducks through shop doorway.

INSIDE SHOP

The shop is small and there's an aroma that is spicy, musty and brassy with a whiff of stale sweat and rotting fruit. Shelves are stuffed with sweets and savouries, tobacco, prayer mats, cooking oils, bottles of cordial and medicines, newspapers, magazines, music cassettes, videos and brass wear.

Hamid is putting the fresh newspapers on display when the shop doorbell rings, two women enter wearing long skirts and headscarves and they wander round the shop ignoring him. Hamid goes behind the counter and pulls open a drawer. It's nearly empty except for a pack of rubber bands, a stapler and a broken door handle. The drawer is lined with brown paper; he lifts up the liner and extracts two posters from underneath. He smoothes them on the counter top. They're photocopies on coloured A4 paper and have dirty old blu-tack stuck on their corners. Hamid sticks them on the glass shop door facing on to the street.

ORIENTAL DANCE
CLASSES FOR WOMEN

BELLY DANCE
SEVEN VEILS
RAQS SHARQI

WEDNESDAY & SATURDAY
9,00 pm to 10,30 pm

First lesson free. Come along with a friend.

LIBRARY AUDITORIUM, 12
VICTORIA ROAD

Call: Dance Master Hamid
222 654 197

The second poster is written in Persian and English.

LADIES ARE YOU TIRED OF STRUGGLING TO UNDERSTAND ENGLISH?

HOW DO YOU GET GOOD SERVICE?

NEED TO HELP YOUR CHILDREN WITH SCHOOL HOMEWORK?

*Gentlewoman, retired Persian widow, is willing to visit you in your own home, to instruct you in
the art of English language and literature.*

**Please enquire to my son:
Mr Reza Mahammed Al hajj
222 897 562**

INSIDE SHOP

Hamid is sitting on a stool behind the counter; he takes two mobile phones out of his jacket, one is red the other's yellow.

The door opens and a couple walk in, Zina and Jamshid Mohamed, Hamid watches them as they walk around the shop. Jamshid has a beard of tangled, frizzled hairs like pubic hair, wild and wiry. His moustache sprouts under his nose like a matted bush growing around his fat wet lips. Lips red like labia, like an unshaved vagina, right there, right on his face.

The two women come over and put down some tins of biscuits on the counter. Hamid starts totalling them on the cash register. Jamshid has gone over to the newspaper rack and Zina stands next to him in her long black coat and black headscarf. She stares hard at Hamid as he hands the change to the two women.

When they leave she approaches Hamid.

Zina: Are you having ghee?

Hamid: Yes, let me show you our selection.

Hamid pushes past Zina to lead the way to a shelf stacked with cooking ingredients. She doesn't try to move out of his way instead she wills her breasts to swell like two large ripe melons so he'll have to brush against them. He passes her a bottle of ghee oil and she takes it, her hand closing over Hamid's fingers.

Zina: *(Low voice.)* You see I come?

Hamid: *(Low voice.)* I've been waiting. I thought you'd changed your mind.

Zina: *(Low voice.)* I here, see! *(She holds the bottle out in front of her, inspecting it.)* I carry my husband here.

Hamid: Well done! *(Hamid takes back the bottle and holds another one out to her.)* This one perhaps?

Hamid watches her, his eyes narrow, his chest heaves. Zina in a trance, intoxicated by the scent of molasses and

23

sweat, her mouth slightly open, takes a breath and steps forward reaching for the bottle.

Zina: Yes, this is good.

Hamid holds onto it for a second before letting go and she clutches the bottle to her chest. The telephone suddenly rings and she walks away over to her husband. Hamid chats on the phone while Zina's husband Jamshid stands reading the headlines, then he comes over to the counter with his newspaper and Zina follows behind with her bottle of ghee.

Hamid: OK, I'll call you tomorrow. *(Hamid puts down the telephone and takes the bottle and newspaper, putting them into a bag.)* That's six pounds twenty.

Jamshid pays and checks his change carefully. He has a little women's purse with a clip top for keeping coins. While he's doing this Hamid smiles over his shoulder at Zina who is standing close to the door. They leave and from inside the shop Hamid watches as Zina draws her husband's attention to one of the posters. Jamshid comes back in the shop while Zina waits in the street looking at the window display. Hamid on Jamshid's re-entry busily sorts through a pile of invoices.

Jamshid: Excuse me. Are you knowing the woman who is offering English lessons? *(Hamid raises his eyebrows questioningly.)* I am seeing the poster on the door.

Hamid: Yes of course, her son is a friend of mine. She's a very cultured lady. *(Low voice.)* She's a widow.

Jamshid: Is she expensive?

Hamid: Oh no! I believe her rates are quite reasonable.

Jamshid: Right, well, thank you.

Jamshid leaves the shop. Hamid watches him go with a smug grin on his face.

INSIDE SHOP STOREROOM

It's nearly lunchtime and the radio is on. Hamid is sitting in a sun lounger surrounded by brooms, buckets and cardboard boxes. He's smoking a cigarette and reading a novel, there's a can of beer perched on a box, which he swigs on from time to time.

The radio announces its 1pm. He gets up slowly still reading and then throws his book down on the sun lounger. He turns off the radio, stubs his cigarette out on the floor and goes back through to the shop.

INSIDE SHOP

He's at the door turning the open sign to closed and taking down the two posters. He carries them to the counter, opens the drawer and hides them again under the paper lining. He puts a tape in the cassette player and turns the volume up high, conjuring by magic in his mind a mythical Houri with wide and beautiful eyes like a wild cow.

He extends his arms high above his head, snapping his fingers, cracks sound like pistol shots. He begins to dance slowly across the shop floor until he stands nearly against her. He gyrates his body slowly becoming a bullfighter, his red cape swirling in the air. She slightly raises her skirts above her ankles and paws her daintily shod foot in the sand. She stamps her feet and her nostrils flare. She snorts then drops her head and charges. 'Olè' the red cape like a thunder clap snaps in the air creating a sharp sweet wind that blows her hair around her face and Hamid is spinning like a dervish around her. On and on the click clack tapping of their heels beat up a faster rhythm. Flapping his wings, grazing her flesh, in a boozed trance he performs a mating dance.

PATTY'S FLAT/DAY
BEDROOM

Patty Mcluskey has a double bed with a furry nylon leopard print cover. An elephant and a monkey have been pushed between the headboard and the wall, their torsos flopping forwards, and when she lies in bed these glass eyed creatures stare down on her.

They give comfort to Patty at night when their eyes catch the light from the streetlamps outside the window.

There's a fake zebra skin on the floor and a group of cheap plastic baby dolls sit on the dressing table. In front of the window is a painting easel and small round bar table loaded with oil paints and jam jars.

Patty Mcluskey is in her thirties, she dresses in thigh high stiletto boots and hot pants and has shaggy peroxide blonde hair.

The best is her mouth, which droops, sulky and puckered in the centre waiting to kiss, her eyes slant away at the corners covering secrets.

She is dancing in front of the mirror to a song on the radio. Holding a paintbrush in one hand and a cigarette in the other she shimmies and spins singing out the words. The deejay cuts in, the music stops and Patty goes back to her easel.

Pinned on the canvas is a photograph of a sullen young man. Below are the beginnings of his portrait, his head like an egg, and his face the same puce pink as the cheap plastic dolls. She stands mixing some brown to tone it down, stabbing with her paintbrush, defining his jaw and cheeks, giving the appearance of huge eye bags.

Patty: Now it's coming, that's it!

She takes a deep drag on her cigarette, eyes narrowed as she looks at the portrait through exhaled smoke. Sitting on the bed flicking through a book on Matisse she stops at a portrait entitled André Derain painted in bold unlikely hues. She stares hard, slams the book shut then bounces up and dashes back to her easel. She squeezes out some acid green and slashes away at his forehead creating a wild network of stalks and gashes then she stands back and giggles.

Patty: Yeah, brilliant!

She looks in wonderment at her act of creation, a man of sour pink and green. The painting grows in her mind's eye entangled with the stalky brambles across his forehead. She hears the front door open. Patty's boyfriend Pete appears at the bedroom door, he looks pissed off.

Pete: Aren't you ready?

Patty: Yeah, look at me! *(She lifts up her arms to present herself in a Hollywood diva style, an old diva.)* Hey, come and see how your portrait is coming along.

Pete walks into the room unconvinced. He stares at the painting. He thinks it's crap, and he's insulted as it looks nothing like his photograph. She has painted him sort of ugly and weird and not good looking or handsome or anything like that, and she's off her face and a waste of space. He turns to look at Patty who's standing with her legs apart, exhaling smoke. He looks her slowly up and down and doesn't like what he sees.

Pete: Look, are you gonna get ready or not? I'm leaving in ten minutes.

Patty: I am ready. *(She turns away to stick her paintbrush in a jar of turpentine.)*

Pete: You're not coming with me dressed like that.

Patty: Why not, what's wrong with me?

Pete: *(Resigned.)* You look like a fucking Christmas tree.

Patty: Christmas tree? Why?

Pete: You just do, you're like mutton dressed as lamb, you're not sixteen, when are you gonna learn? *(He turns on his heel and goes out the door into the hall.)*

Patty: OK, OK, wait I'll get changed. *(She runs to the bedroom door and leans out holding onto the frame.)*

STAIRWAY TO FRONT DOOR

Coming down the flight of stairs she's now dressed like Pete in jeans and leather jacket.

Patty: You didn't even say what you thought of my painting.

Pete: Don't start again.

Patty: At least tell me, do you like it or not?

Pete: No! It's a fucking mess, looks like a thick kid or a blind man painted it.

Pete pushes past Patty to go through the door first, she follows him out.

BABAI FLAT/DAY

CORRIDOR

(Mid afternoon the following day.) Hamid kicks open the door. He's carrying a scruffy Jack Russell dog in his arms. The old man comes to the sitting room doorway.

Old man: What is this? Put it down and kick it out the door, then wash your shoe seven times. Oh my God you must wash all seven times! Hands, jacket, everything! You fool! How many times have I told you, never touch a dog…. Get it out!

Hamid: *(Kicking the door shut behind him.)* Dad listen! I can't, I've saved him! Some bastard tied him to a lamp post across the road from the shop and abandoned him.

Old Man: I don't care what some other bloody bastard did! You are not bringing a dog in the house. Oh no! You tried many times as a boy, now you think I am old and gaga? Take it back where you found it!

Hamid: I can't Dad, he won't do any harm.

Old man: Everyone knows the Angel Gabriel will not enter any home with a dog inside!

Hamid: Angel Gabriel doesn't visit us, even if we don't have a dog!

Old man: How do you know what the Angel Gabriel does? Dogs can't be in the house or he won't enter and that's the truth! What is all this rescuing and saving dogs? What is wrong with your brains? *(He snaps his fingers in front of Hamid's eyes.)*

Hamid: Listen, when I found him I took him to the Dogs Home. It's a dog's hell and they told me if no one adopted him he'd be put down. *(Shakes his head.)* So I had to save him! He's a great dog; he'll make a great pet.

Old man: You can't keep it as a pet because that's the custom of the bloody Kafirs, and what is this adoption rubbish, adopt a dog? Nonsense! Is he a human orphan? There's no reason to keep a dog as a pet, it's a waste of time.

Hamid: Why not? What's wrong with him? Look at him! *(Hamid holds the dog out to the old man who recoils backwards.)* I've named him Turpin after the famous highwayman.

Old man: *(The old man takes a quick glance at Turpin, who's looking most sorrowful.)* It is not permissible for a Muslim to keep a dog. If people are praying and a dog walks within a stones throw of them, their prayer is made null and void. Listen Idiot! You can only have a dog if you are blind or deaf. Whoever keeps a dog loses the rewards for his good deeds! *(Turpin lets out a pitiful howl.)* Unless of course the dog is used for guarding a farm or cattle.

Hamid: That's it! We need a guard dog, rising crime in the area and all that, he'll be useful.

Old man: Don't talk rot! Look at him! A guard dog my arse! He's no bigger than a cat!

Hamid: He'll grow! He's intelligent, he'll bark if robbers try and break in!

Old man: *(Narrowing his eyes, peering more closely.)* At least he's not black. Black dogs are the devil in animal form. All black dogs must be killed! They are the dogs of Satan, hmm; he has a black patch over his eye that is a bad sign!

Hamid: Kill Scooby Doo? Kill Lassie?

Old man: Of course not! *(Throwing up his arms.)* Are you blind? I have seen Lassie myself on the telly, and that stupid Scooby Doo and they are not black!

SITTING ROOM/NIGHT

Later that evening, Faruzeh, Abbas and Hosro are sitting round the table finishing dinner. Hamid is lying on the sofa. Turpin is lying on Hamid's stomach watching his face with raptured love. Hamid has a cushion on his head, shading his eyes from the glaring ceiling lights.
'Cathedral chandelier in satin nickel finish.' The old man had told Hamid.
'Dad it'll bring the ceiling down!'
The old man went on. 'It has three tiers with nine arms and one thousand watts.'
The old man sits for hours every day under his cathedral lights, a wizened being, his old dry stick bones and leathered skin basking in the brilliant light like the sun, and he dreams how long ago the air had once been full of light, closer to the sky with endless horizons.

Abbas: I've had it with him, where is he anyway?

Faruzeh: Ohh…. He'll be at the mosque.

Abbas: I wish he'd fucking go and live there.

Faruzeh: HOSRO! Don't pick your pimples at the table.

Abbas: He's always clearing his phlegm, belching and farting.

Hosro: I don't.

Faruzeh: Don't be smart!

Abbas: *(Still oblivious to his son and wife.)* He's getting worse by the day, I can't stand it! Those prayers every bloody morning, he's even kicked a hole in the bedroom door.

Hosro: He hasn't, it's just dented.

Faruzeh: HOSRO! Who asked you to butt in? Go and finish your homework, NOW! *(Hosro saunters out.)*

Abbas: How many times have I trodden on his syringes in my bare feet? I ask you? I sat on one too the other day. I got the needle stuck in my arse, it snapped and I had to go to Casualty. Just think! I had to wait three hours because they said it wasn't an emergency, and I couldn't even sit down.

Faruzeh is laughing at him and his face gets redder.

Abbas embraces all that is Japanese. He wears Happi coats decorated with bamboo and dragons, and T-shirts with Japanese characters embroidered on the back saying 'Good will.' and 'Long life.'

Tonight with the old man out the way he's wearing his favourite clothes. This fatty bucked toothed man in his Japanese silk kimono, his Geta wooden Japanese flip flops on high wooden blocks, his frizzy hair, drenched in oil and tied up in the true samurai topknot. He's like a tired and beaten old warrior with no sword and no respect, just industrial sushi that's cheaper the day before its expiry date.

Abbas: Stop laughing, I've really had it this time. I'm going to the estate agents tomorrow, we're moving out.

Faruzeh: You always say that.

Abbas: Why not? All the money we've put by and Hosro doesn't even have his own room.

Faruzeh: That's for Hosro's future and you've already bought us one house, remember? In bloody Wimbledon with a sitting tenant who won't bloody die.

Abbas: It was a great deal at half the market value, it was all we could afford and she's past eighty.

Faruzeh: Some people live to be a hundred.

Abbas: I'll rent us somewhere.

Faruzeh: Yeah do that! More money down the drain and
 you know we'll have to take Dad with us, so what's
 the point? We can't leave him here by himself.
They both look over at Hamid on the sofa with the
cushion on his head. He waves at them.
Hamid: We all need our own room, don't worry! Hosro
 will be off to some university in a year and I'll take
 care of Dad.
Abbas: *(To Hamid.)* Can you give me a cigarette?
Hamid comes over to the table and sits down. He offers
his packet first to Abbas and then to Faruzeh. They sit
together blowing smoke and saying nothing. Abbas puts
his leftover dinner down on the floor.
Abbas: Here Turpin, come on boy! *(Turpin bounds over his
 tail wagging and licks the plate clean.)*
Faruzeh: Don't let Dad catch you! *(Turns to Hamid.)*
 Didn't he tell you to take the dog back where you
 found him?
Hamid: Can't remember, he said a lot of things. Do you
 want to stay here Turpin? *(Smiles nodding at Turpin.)*
 Yes you do! Don't you?

JAMSHID'S FLAT SITTING ROOM/NIGHT
Jamshid's father is sitting asleep on a large leather sofa.
Next to the sofa is Jamshid's mother, a tiny old woman in
a wheelchair. She's been parked carelessly and is actually
facing the wall. She's awake and has a tray of food
balanced on the arms of her wheelchair. Jamshid is sitting
on a leather-upholstered wing chair with his feet up on a
pouf. He's watching the television, which is fitted into a
vinyl unit together with a decoder and DVD player. Next
to him on the coffee table are three remote controls. Zina
is clearing the dining table behind him and then she
moves over to Jamshid's mother and checks her tray. She
picks up the plate and starts pushing spoonfuls of rice
into the old woman's mouth without paying attention.

The old woman is gaga and dribbles her food back out while Zina watches Jamshid's back.

Zina: Jamshid…. Jamshid, you are saying tonight you calling madam English teacher!

Jamshid: I'm watching the news.

Zina: Yes and after news is you want be millionaire man, then more news, then is very late.

Jamshid: Damn! OK! *(He turns round, annoyed.)* And stop feeding my maman, look she is full! *(He starts flicking his remote controls one in each hand and sends the volume up too high.)* Damn! *(He turns off the volume.)* Bring me number and phone.

Zina puts the plate down and goes over to the sideboard. She picks up the cordless phone and takes a small notebook from Jamshid's jacket. She carries them over and holds them out under his nose; Jamshid is staring at the news with no audio.

BABAI FLAT SITTING ROOM/NIGHT

Faruzeh and Abbas are watching a variety show on the television. Hamid is playing chess with Hosro when a phone rings. He pulls the red and the yellow cell phone out of his pocket; the red one is ringing and he answers.

Hamid: Good evening…. Yes speaking…. Oh right, I understand, would you mind waiting one moment? *(Hamid gets up, puts the yellow phone back in his pocket and grabs a pen, and then he pauses wondering if he's forgotten something. He turns to Hosro.)* I'll be back in a minute; it's a private call. *(He looks down at the board.)* Don't move ehh!

JAMSHID'S FLAT SITTING ROOM/NIGHT

Jamshid is sitting with the telephone held out like a sceptre. Zina is standing behind him, her hand resting on the top of his winged chair like a royal portrait photo.

Jamshid's mother is forgotten still turned towards the wall, while his father sleeps on with his mouth open.

Jamshid: He's gone to fetch his mother to the phone. *(He replaces the phone next to his ear and waits, and then there is the faint sound of a female voice on the line.)* I have sawn your advertisement for English lessons and I'm wanting some more information.... Not for me, for my wife.

Hamid: *(On the phone, speaking with a falsetto female voice.)* Does your wife speak any English?

Jamshid: Yes, very very badly, always mistakes, no grasping of grammar. But worse! While she can gabble some English she can't read the Roman alphabet letters, she wants to help the children with this school homework.... You can give private lessons at home?

Hamid: *(On the phone, female voice.)* I'm free on Tuesday and Thursday afternoons, I charge fifteen pounds per lesson.

Jamshid: I think one lesson a week enough, but what about your teaching methods, are you using the full immersion?

BABAI FLAT BATHROOM/NIGHT
Hamid's in the bathroom sitting on the toilet lid. He's talking on the red telephone in a high-pitched old woman's voice.

Hamid: Oh yes! I believe in full immersion, most definitely. I never speak in Persian, unless it's absolutely necessary. Apart from general grammar and learning our ABC we also recite passages from the classics like Shakespeare, Milton and so on. It improves the vocabulary and diction.... *(While he's saying this, he also changes his facial expressions and posture. Drawing himself up with dignity he purses his mouth and narrows his eyes to become an old widow sitting on a toilet. He* *pats his imaginary coiffure into place.)* Tuesday? . . . Fine, could you give me your address? *(He scribbles it down.)* Yes, thank you, four o'clock.... Good-bye.

Hamid switches off the phone, smiles and flushes the toilet. He winks at the Spanish toilet roll cover doll.

JAMSHID'S FLAT SITTING ROOM/NIGHT

Jamshid is sitting holding out the telephone for Zina to take away.

Jamshid: Mind you, as I'm paying for these lessons, I don't want to hear you on the phone to Tehran chitter chattering with your friends. I'm not throwing any more money down the loo.... *(Jamshid turns the television back up.)*

PATTY'S FLAT/NIGHT

KITCHEN

Patty's sitting at the table in a gloomy neon light. She tips up her glass and drains it. There's an empty bottle of Pernod on the table and she's drunk.

Patty: *(Mumbling to herself.)* Swami Pete, life dedicated to watering plants and doing naked yoga, and never forgets to pick up his pocket money from his mum. *(Changes voice.)* And when my mates turn up he just ponces right on into the kitchen, wearing a pair of tight bloody Y fronts, just to show off his big cock coiled up like a snake.... Ha ha! *(Patty starts giggling and lights a cigarette.)*

SPARE BEDROOM

Pete's sitting at a large office desk reading a book by the light of the outside street lamp. The room's lined with odd wardrobes and piles of boxes. Patty walks in leaving the door open behind her; Pete ignores her.

Patty: What ya doin? *(Pete doesn't answer he keeps reading.)* Is that book any good? *(She leans forward.)* Ah, it's the one

35

about that Sadhu, the one who turned kites into chocolate bars. *(She looks at Pete and then starts laughing.)* Ha ha…. *(She trips forward on the desk her tits half out. He's still staring hard at the book but she knows he's listening.)* Hmm . . . d'you remember that fortune-teller woman? The one who was a man and then turned into a woman after she met Sai Baba…. You remember? *(Pete doesn't answer nor look at her.)* You wanna watch that doesn't happen to you…. *(She starts giggling again.)*

Pete: I'm off. *(He stands up and shuts his book.)*

Patty: Where're you going? *(She stretches over the desk and squeezes his crotch.)*

Pete: To my mum's, leave it…. *(He pushes Patty's hand away.)*

Patty: Just joking…. Oh come on, don't go!

Pete: I can't talk to you, can I? You don't get it! On a spiritual level it's like a Ferrari and a 50cc moped, I don't need this!

Patty: So what are you? A Ferrari?

Pete goes out closing the door, shutting Patty in the room behind him, leaving her in the dark.

BABAI FLAT SITTING ROOM/DAY

(A few days later.) Hosro is sitting at the dining table eating breakfast and little Turpin is sitting on the floor next to his chair watching his every move. Hosro throws him toast crusts and he stands up on his back legs and gobbles them up. The old man comes through the doorway.

Old man: Down Turpin! Hosro, dog's saliva is dirty so you can't let it lick you or get its wet fur on your clothes. The animal is a fool.

Hosro: Oh Grandad, look at him, watch him catch this! *(Hosro tosses a crust in the air and Turpin leaps up and snap, it's gone.)*

Old man: Better than a Hoover! But you know a little puppy once stopped an angel from entering a house because it was unclean, and if you touch a dog you must wash seven times. It is wrong! This Turpin is a rascal and a bad influence. We should send him to one of those Dog Homes.

Turpin looks with his glowing soft brown eyes at the old man when he says this, as though he understands perfectly and he hangs his head in shame.

Hosro: Look Baba you're upsetting his feelings!

Old man: Don't be ridiculous! No one listens to me in this house. How can a dog listen? It has no brains.

He stomps over to the armchair and sits down. Hosro gets up and takes his breakfast tray out to the kitchen and Turpin sits quietly watching the old man who ignores him.

The letterbox clacks open and shut and Turpin races out into the hall skidding on the tiles. He trots back in with a newspaper in his jaws. He knows very well to bring it to the old man.

Old man: Tsk tsk, now you've defiled my newspaper with your saliva. *(He inspects the newspaper.)* Hmm just a bit damp. *(He looks at Turpin.)* All right, all right, sit! *(He waves his hand at Turpin like a priest giving benediction.)*

MARKET/DAY

Patty is walking through the market. She'd like to stop at every stall and buy everything, the kid gloves, the felt hats and belts with silver buckles. The men on the stalls watch her, knowing she wants to try on every skirt and dress and wear every chain and pendant. Until, like a mad bag lady swaddled in a hundred layers of clothes, her neck weighed down by a thousand necklaces, she will fall to the ground and crawl through the streets, while her gold crucifixes and jade beads drag through the dust.

She's been shopping all her life, her cupboards and wardrobes are crammed full with everything she's ever bought and never worn or used. Bolts of material, saris and kaftans and cocktail dresses and ball gowns, but the most secret is a silk wedding dress as white as snow.

INSIDE SHOP/DAY

Hamid's in the shop drinking a beer behind the counter and tapping his feet to a song on the cassette player. In walks Patty Mcluskey. She smiles at Hamid and wanders over to the shelf displays. Hamid watches her as she walks around. She gets some rose oil and a narghile and takes them over to the counter. Hamid is looking intently at Patty. She notices and feels excited.

Patty: Uhh . . . can you tell me how this works? I've only seen them in the movies. *(She looks expectantly at Hamid.)*

Hamid: Well, you fill this part with water, and here you put the tobacco, and then you draw the smoke through here. *(Patty's watching his hands as they touch the narghile.)*

Patty: And then the water bubbles?

Hamid: Yes.

Patty: And is it cool to smoke?

Hamid: Very cool. *(He's smiling now.)* When I was a kid my grandmother had one . . . she kept tiny dolls in the water to amuse us, they bounced around when she smoked.

Patty: Wow! Oh, I want some tiny dolls too, have you got any?

Hamid: *(Laughs.)* No, that was just my grandmother.

Two women walk into the shop, Amina, Hamid's dance class partner and her friend Carla.

Patty: Tobacco?

Hamid: Over there. *(He points.)*

Patty wanders around the shop while Hamid talks to his friends. He's in a hurry for them to leave.

Amina: Salaam Hamid….

Hamid: Hey! A surprise visit?

Amina: Want to have a coffee with us?

Hamid: Can't! My sister won't be in till after lunch.

Carla: Oh, come on. Just shut the shop for five minutes.

Hamid: Can't.

Amina: Well, we're going for a wander. Shame you can't come. *(She winks at Hamid.)* See you tomorrow and bring some new music.

As Hamid's friends leave the shop they look curiously at Patty who has come back over to the counter.

Patty: I saw there's a belly dance class on the door there. Is it a friend of yours?

Hamid: No, actually it's me. *(He smiles.)*

Patty: Really? I love dancing. I might come one evening.

Hamid: Here let me give you a music cassette. *(He rummages through the cassettes.)* My present, take it home.

Patty: No, I couldn't really.

Hamid: Please, it's only a copy. I make copies for my friends.

Hamid slides it across the counter, and Patty fumbles putting it in her bag. She's embarrassed by Hamid's intense stare, then Hamid starts totalling up the rose oil, tobacco packets and the narghile.

BABAI FLAT SITTING ROOM/NIGHT
It's early evening; Faruzeh is laying the table and Abbas is spraying air freshener. Hosro is hoovering under the table, then he turns off the Hoover.

Hosro: Do I have to go to the mosque with Baba? Please?

Faruzeh: Yes! It's all arranged, he's coming back to get you any minute.

Hosro: It's not fair. Please can't you tell him I'm sick? I'll stay in my room. I promise I won't bother you, oh go on....

Abbas: I don't see why he can't stay here?

Faruzeh: *(Exasperated.)* If he doesn't take Hosro to evening prayers, he'll be praying on the floor here in the middle of dinner.

Abbas: Please Hosro? Look, I'll give you extra pocket money to spend with your friends on Saturday to make up for it.

Hosro: OK. *(Big sigh, he switches the Hoover back on.)*

The old man and Hosro have secrets. When Hosro was a little boy with chubby knees and still had fat on the back of his hands, the old man loved putting him to bed at night. He would tell him the legends of Sinbad the sailor, Persian fairy stories with djinns and ghouls and the tales of mullah Nazruddin. But what they both loved best were the jokes, mostly the jokes about Abbas and his huge buck teeth.

The old man would ask little Hosro. 'Why does your mother make your father Abbas stand in the hall when she has a dinner party?' Hosro would pretend not to know. 'So her guests can hang their coats on his teeth.' And they got worse. 'Why did Abbas's mother stick his head down the toilet and flush?' They both began to giggle. 'She used his teeth to scrape the pooh off the toilet rim.' And the best one. 'What does Abbas use for a toothbrush?' They both knew. 'A loo brush.'

Hosro had clapped his hands, eyes shiny and cheeks red like apples, he was sweeter than sugar and the old man was overwhelmed by his love.

Now Hosro was skinny and secretive and the old man missed that little boy like hell, it was as though he'd gone away and died and the old man wanted him back.

SELMA'S HOUSE/NIGHT
SITTING ROOM

There are four men sitting crowded round the television, Selma's husband Amjad, her brother Koosha and her two sons.

Amjad is wearing an open Hawaiian shirt, shorts and flip-flops. He has his feet up on the coffee table. Koosha, in his late 20's is puffy and bloated, with lacquered hair and plenty of gold jewellery. The two boys are huge and strapping, wearing sports clothes with designer names printed everywhere. They all wear Baseball caps pulled down over their brows hiding their eyes, making their mouths sinister.

The table is loaded with drink cans and ashtrays. All four are smoking and stuffing themselves with crisps and pistachios. They're watching a league football match on the television and shouting a bit.

Amjad: COME ON . . . YEAH GO! . . . SHIT!

Koosha: Bastard, GO . . . NO!

Amjad: NAH!

Son one: GOAL GOAL!

The doorbell rings, they freeze for a moment and stop shouting.

Amjad: It's Maman's teacher, go on, go and let her in.

Son two: *(He gives his father a suffering look.)* Oh, I'm gonna miss a goal. *(He shuffles off to open the door, and then he comes back in followed by Hamid who can't be recognised. Hamid is wearing a black burqa, black gloves, white socks and sandals, and he's carrying a large sports bag.)* Uh... Maman is in the bedroom.

Hamid nods slightly and walks out of the sitting room to the corridor. Koosha looks over his shoulder at Hamid.

Koosha: Is that Selma's teacher?

Amjad: Yeah, she's an old widow.

Son one: Old crow!

Amjad: Shut your face and don't be rude.

41

Koosha: *(Slapping his thigh.)* Yeah! GOAL….

They carry on watching the match, swigging and eating. They shout their heads off and dream they are there scoring goals. The boys dream of fighting each other like wild dogs over a bone or a bitch. They'll sniff a bitch's flanks and mount her from behind. They are strong hard boys and they will rabbit punch their rivals.

SELMA'S BEDROOM.

Selma is standing at a dressing table covered with exercise books and a big dictionary.

Plugged into the wall near the door is a cassette player on the floor. The door opens, in walks the strangest creature draped in an old widow's dusty burqa. A sheer greying veil hangs stretched across its face like a creepy ghoul. The stuff of nightmares as the creature shuffles across the room reeking of wet wood and mothballs.

Hamid: *(Falsetto.)* Have you done your homework exercises Selma?

Selma: Yes, of course.

Hamid: *(Falsetto.)* Good girl you're one of my best students!

Hamid puts his bag down and takes out a cassette. He kneels down and removes his gloves revealing his chubby childish hands. He puts the cassette in and presses play, then slowly turns up the volume. There is a recorded woman's voice reciting phrases.

'I AM PLAYING, I WAS PLAYING, ARE YOU PLAYING? PLAY WITH ME!

I AM SINGING, I WAS SINGING….'

The tape is playing an English lesson. His burqa falls down around his feet and he steps out wearing red jockey briefs. He kicks his sandals away and he's all stripped down. He's become Selma's short thick-bodied demon lover with his snow white socks on. Now there's an aroma of wild black cherries in the air. He watches her

42

undress, spinning in a yellow-bedroom light, her black curls tangled in a slowly dipping halo. Her bare feet with painted toenails dance on the burqa next to Hamid's feet.

BABAI FLAT SITTING ROOM/NIGHT

(Later, on the same evening.) Faruzeh and Abbas are sitting at the dining table with another couple, Sadam and Sepideh. They pass around steaming hot dishes of delicious food. Abbas holds his head back and really laughs, his huge yellow teeth gleaming in the candlelight. They toast each other with bittersweet wine and Faruzeh is flushed a vermillion red. Some Persian pop music is playing. Sadam and Sepideh clap their hands as Abbas dances, dressed tonight in full regalia, in his high heeled wooden Geta, twirling in his long silk kimono. His samurai top knot falls down and he falls into Faruzeh's lap. She passes him the bottle, he blows in her ear and they really love each other. They chuck savoury rice balls across the carpet for Turpin while Sadam and Sepideh brush hands and touch feet under the table while feeding each other with delicate morsels. They gossip and giggle. Faruzeh brings a fruit tart to the table balanced on her head, and there are still two bottles of wine amidst the leftovers from their dinner. A banging noise starts in the hall but no one seems to notice except Turpin, who runs out the room skidding into the hall, his tail wagging.

Abbas: I can't believe it, how old is she?

Sepideh: About forty I'd say.

Faruzeh: And can't his mother stop him?

Sepideh: She's tried everything. She stopped his pocket money and then he moved out, and now he's living with her.

Abbas: Hooey! She must be old enough to be . . . *(Strangled voice.)* his mother.

The old man has walked straight into the sitting room followed by a sheepish Hosro. The table freezes and conversation stops while the old man strides across the room. He doesn't notice the dinner and he goes over to the windows and throws them open.

Old man: The boy wanted to come home, says he feels sick. It's stuffy in here the air is no good! No good air is bad for the brain.

While the old man is opening the windows Abbas whips up the wine bottles. He goes to the wall unit and quickly pulls down a framed picture of a holy sage. He shoves the bottles on the shelf and hurriedly replaces the picture in front of them. He doesn't notice he's put the holy sage back upside down.

Faruzeh: Hosro?

Hosro: I can't help it if I feel sick. *(He looks ashamed and guilty.)* I'm going to bed.

Old man: *(Calling to Hosro.)* Bring my insulin I need a shot!

Faruzeh is panic-stricken and she sinks down in her chair. Abbas sits down too, his face is grey.

Abbas: Do you remember Sadam? And Sepideh?

Old man: Yes, my pleasure. *(Pointing his finger at Sadam.)* You're the one that married that fatty beautiful girl. *(He comes forward scanning the table. Sadam stands up while Sepideh stays in her seat.)*

Old man: *(Leaning forward, looking hard at Sepideh.)* Ehh, your husband not with you?

Meanwhile Hosro has come back in and is waiting with the syringe and insulin behind the old man, he coughs.

Old man: *(Turning round.)* Oh there you are!

The old man sits down on the sofa, pulls his tunic up over his knee, prepares his syringe and jabs his thigh. The two guests are watching while Faruzeh and Abbas wish the shot were arsenic.

SELMA'S HOUSE SITTING ROOM/NIGHT
The football match has finished. There's a quiz show on
the television with the volume turned down low. They
can distinctly hear the English lesson on the cassette
player coming from Selma's bedroom, now reciting
Paradise Lost. Then the woman's voice suddenly stops.
The four men continue watching the show.

Son one: I'm hungry.

Koosha: Me too, look it's past dinner time.

Amjad: Selma is cooking Albaloo Polow tonight. *(He crunches up an empty packet of cigarettes.)*

Koosha: I'll go and get some more fags from the Paki shop.

Hamid comes into the sitting room from the bedroom.
He's fully dressed in his burqa and gloves. He walks
towards them, and Amjad stands up awkwardly trying to
get out from between the coffee table and the sofa. He
blocks Hamid from getting any nearer.

Amjad: Erh! Right, you've finished, I'll just get your money. *(Amjad goes to the sideboard, gets his wallet from the drawer, and takes out 15 pounds and hands it to Hamid.)* And how's my wife coming along?

Hamid: *(Falsetto.)* Oh, she's doing well! She's a very good student.

Amjad: *(Uncomfortable.)* Right, I'll see you out. *(Amjad ambles to the door, lets Hamid through and shuts it.)*

BABAI FLAT SITTING ROOM/NIGHT
Faruzeh and Abbas are seated around the dining table
with Sepideh and Sadam.
The old man is standing on his prayer mat reciting verses
with his back to the table.

Abbas: This tart is delicious.

Faruzeh: Yes, I picked it up from the new bakery next to the shop; I had a hard time choosing.

Sepideh: Have you heard they're opening an ice skating rink at the park?

Abbas: Ice rink? It's not winter yet.

Sepideh: It'll be all year round, refrigerated under a dome.

The old man comes over to the table. He picks up some tart and shoves it in his mouth and starts talking with his mouth full.

Old man: Refrigerated! What a waste of money, tsk, it will be a failure. *(He shakes his head sadly.)* Who'll want to go? *(He shrugs his shoulders.)* Now! *(He jabs his finger at them, then takes a chair and sits down.)* I've been thinking of a plan! A good business, do you know what? A laundry service! Buy some washing machines and some irons. You know with a small investment we could make a lot of business…. Tsk, everybody has dirty washing! Women work, who has time to wash? *(He stuffs more tart in his mouth.)* Huh? Now I've been looking into this laundry business, it's a good thing. Get some machines and then you start.

Abbas: *(Sarcastic.)* Of course, how stupid I am, why on earth didn't I think of it?

Old man: Because you're a fool, born a fool and will always be a fool! Ha ha, it's clear we only need to look at you! And what is this you are wearing tonight? *(He stands up and points at Abbas, his voice rising.)* A lady's dressing gown? What are those wooden contraptions you have upon your feet? My God, what is this? Has my idiot daughter married a sissy boy? A pansy? Oh, don't look shocked, the truth is always the truth.

Faruzeh: Dad, that's enough, finish your prayers. *(Her eyes are burning bright and Abbas is as red as blood.)*

Old man: Finish my prayers? Who are you to tell me what I must do? What do you know of Qiyaam al-Layl? Is it wrong to rest between rak'ahs? If a man is tired from long standing and recitation, he may allow some rest. True believers forsake their beds at night to invoke their lord in fear and hope and you! *(Points his finger at Abbas.)* He who sleeps all night gets up ill natured and lazy!

Abbas: I've become a Buddhist and follow the eightfold path. You're the one who gets up ill natured and lazy.

Old man: You filthy blaggard, what is this Buddhist rot? You were born a Muslim and will always be Muslim, so shut your bloody mouth and stop blaspheming. Who do you think you are? *(He shrugs his shoulders, waving his arms.)* Are you Chinese? I dare say your guts are fat enough to be a Buddha. You want to kill me? How much shame must I carry on my shoulders? *(He walks away from the table and then turns back to face Abbas.)* You are a donkey, that's why you think you're a Buddhist! A Muslim should never give the Quran to a Buddhist; they mistake it for a comic book, with a Mickey Mouse character called Mohammed in it. You're an imbecile just like them!

Sadam: Mr Babai, Sir, Buddha never professed himself a god, so what's the harm?

Old man: Don't you stick your big nose in my family affairs. You are here without your wife and she *(Points to Sepideh.)* is here without her husband. You can't pull the wool over my eyes I know what's going on, in my own house too. *(Points to Faruzeh.)* It's a bad day when an old man comes home from the mosque, he wishes to pray and his prayers are drowned with talk of tarts. Am I disturbing your fine dinner party? Why wasn't I invited? Not even your own son! Why do you arrange all this without your family? *(He looks down under the table and kicks a plate out from underneath across the floor.)* And how many times have I told you not to feed the bloody dog on our PLATES!

The old man storms out the room banging the door. He's ruined their party, squashed them like cockroaches, their tiny shiny shells crushed under the weight of his heavy boot. No one laughs any longer and it's not funny anymore. There's just a dead dull silence.

PATTY'S FLAT SPARE BEDROOM/DAY
(Early afternoon.) Pete is sitting in the dark at the desk in the spare bedroom. The curtains are drawn and he's reading by a thin crack of grey light. The door is shut and Patty is standing outside knocking.
Patty: Pete . . . Pete? *(Pete doesn't answer.)*
Patty opens the door and walks in followed by her friend Melanie. Pete still doesn't look up from his book. It seems as though Patty is showing Melanie a mental case she keeps locked away in a room. They stand staring at him; watching him while he reads on ignoring them. They wait to see what he'll do, ready to run in case he overturns the desk and throws his book at their heads. Slowly they edge closer.
Patty: Pete, Melanie's come over.
Pete: *(Looking up.)* Hello Melanie.
Patty: *(Turning to Melanie.)* Pete's reading about the autobiography of a Yogi! He's doing a lot of yoga too, and meditation, aren't you Pete?
Melanie: You'll ruin your eyes.
Pete shrugs and carries on reading. He's as thin as a whip, all knotted inside, peering through thick glasses that magnify his eyes, like black shining orbs that judge and stare. He's strung so tight he'll snap if they play with him.
Patty: We're having a coffee, want a cup? *(Pete ignores her.)* Oh well, I'll bring you one.
Patty walks out with Melanie, closing the door behind them. Pete can hear them laughing loudly on the other side of the door.

BABAI FLAT SITTING ROOM/DAY

It's mid afternoon and everyone is out except the old man. He's sitting under his thousand-watt chandelier basking in the light. Turpin is sitting on the floor watching the carpet. He lifts his paw up ready to test its softness.

Old man: Don't you dare you rascal! That's my prayer carpet and don't look at me like that, you've been brought up badly and never learned how to behave.... *(He shakes his head.)* Nothing but a delinquent! Tsk tsk!

Turpin runs out the room and returns with the old man's slippers. He drops them down in front of his chair.

Old man: Now you've contaminated these too!

He ignores Turpin and stares out the window at the muddy dirt grey sky. Turpin runs in and out the room amassing a pile of offerings around the old man, Faruzeh's pink fluffy mules, an old newspaper, a carpet brush, a leather handbag and Abbas's wooden platform flip-flops. He watches the old man, waiting, and then he gently paws at his leg.

Old man: What's all this? Did I ask for this rubbish?

Turpin holds out his little paw and the old man in trance reaches out his hand and shakes it solemnly.

Old man: Freezing cold feet! Those imbeciles don't know how to look after you! Do you know Hosro would be dead by now if it weren't for my intervention on numerous occasions? *(He shakes his head, watching Turpin with a solemn stare.)* And what a stupid name 'Turpin!' Who ever heard of a dog named after some idiot highway robber? Now what we need is a name that suits, with the right number it will bring you some luck.

He gets up from the chair and hobbles over to the shelf. Fetching his calculator, pen and paper he sits down at the table.

Old Man: Asad or Behrang? Now! *(He turns to Turpin.)*

Every Arabic letter stands for a number, and we call this Abjad. *(He totals and subtracts.)* Hmm, number one is not good for you! You see it's the sun number, and the rays of the sun will develop character such as arrogance and determination, very bad for a dog I think.

Turpin hangs his head in shame.

Old man. Don't take it to heart. I shall give you the perfect name. *(He taps away on his calculator.)* Peshman Babai? Parviz Babai? No! Bad numbers are two, six and eight! These are the people who are full of problems and unsuccessful. *(More tapping.)* I have it, Cyrus! Yes it has the perfect number! Now follow me.

The old man makes his way to the kitchen with the dog following him, and there underneath the neon light the old man presents him with a gift. Turpin Cyrus Babai wags his tail and gobbles down a boxful of Naan Berenji biscuits.

Old man: Hah! Now that's proper stuff, not scraps, you see? Your name is working for you already!

ROAD/NIGHT

(The dance class night.) Patty is on her moped. The street lamps are dripping raindrops and the road shines with puddles. There's an odour of wet tarmac, wet grass, wet dirt. She turns into a side street and parks in the driveway of the community hall. She waits for a while before going inside, smoking a cigarette perched on her moped making her mind up.

INSIDE DANCE CLASS/NIGHT

Inside the hall there are 'No Smoking' signs and posters. Everything is bathed in a strong fluorescent light and it all looks shiny and greasy. Stacked chairs and tables have been pushed together at one end of the hall making room for the dance class.

There is loud Afghani Pashai music playing. Hamid and his teaching partner Amina are dancing facing their students. The women copy the steps and movements made by Amina and Hamid, like crested paradise birds through a looking glass. Performing an elaborate mating dance the birds mirror each other, breast-to-breast, bill-to-bill. They're swinging their hips to the figure of eight, rhythmically with one-foot forward. Amina begins moving her hands, first in a soldier's salute, then to her shoulder, then flinging her arm out, everyone copies. Amina throws out both arms and shakes her shoulders and breasts, her lips puckered, and they all mirror her. Patty appears behind the dancers. She puts her bag down on a bench and stands watching.

Hamid sees Patty and dances towards her, jerking his pelvis, holding out his arms and snapping his fingers. Patty begins to laugh at him. Hamid pulls her towards him gyrating his hips. Embarrassed at first Patty dances by his side following him, and her face is flushed and excited.

Amina juts her head forward and weaves her hands in front of her face, making a spell, invoking a djinn. They all mirror her hands, her eyes, her pout. She sticks her teeth out and covers her bottom lip her eyelids half closed, and every one copies.

OUTSIDE DANCE CLASS/NIGHT

The dance students are coming out of the entrance chatting together. They walk away out on to the street. Hamid, who's slightly concealed in the doorway, walks over to the driveway gates and squats down hiding from the women on the other side of Patty's moped.

He pulls the spark plug cap off, detaching the wire, then he stands back up and slowly makes his way from the shadows back into the light. As the women walk away Hamid saunters back to the doorway. Amina and Patty come out. Amina locks the doors and Patty walks towards her moped.

Patty: I had a good time, it's brilliant.

Hamid: So you're coming again?

Patty: Maybe!

Amina: *(Calling to them as she walks away.)* See you Hamid, bye Patty.

Hamid walks slowly away towards his car. The road is deserted. Patty is sitting astride her moped.

Patty: SHIT!

The moped won't start, so she gets off and begins using the kick-start as Hamid walks back towards her.

Hamid: Problem?

Patty: My moped won't start! *(She keeps trying to kick start it.)*

Hamid: Look, why don't you leave it here tonight and I'll come back in the morning with my toolbox, it's probably the carburettor or the spark plugs. I'm good at fixings motors, give me your number and I'll call you tomorrow when I've got it going.

Patty: Yeah OK, thanks, I'll just park it up.

Hamid takes the moped from her and pushes it onto the grass verge beside the driveway.

Hamid: Let me give you a lift home.

ROAD OUTSIDE PATTY'S FLAT/NIGHT

Patty and Hamid are parked in the road under a streetlamp. She's all orange and grey and when he looks at her she looks away. He reaches out and strokes his fingertips over the white daisies on her blouse. He touches her breast, she looks back up at him. Hamid swallows hard then puts his hand inside her blouse and their eyes meet. Passing car headlights shine in through the darkness flooding the car interior; igniting their bodies like moonbeams licking across their pale skins in a flash and then gone, leaving them again in the murky orange grey light. He slides his hand down inside her trousers.

BABAI FLAT SITTING ROOM/DAY
(Sunday morning.) The old man is walking around the sitting room muttering and counting his prayer beads through his fingers. He sits down at the table next to Hamid who's eating his breakfast.
He unfolds an Islamic comic paper for children, the sort that have moral tales about the lives of wise men with pictures to colour in and quizzes to do.
He flicks through the comic and finds a half finished crossword puzzle. He's already answered a few of the clues. He checks his answers, his pen poised in the air, and then he underlines a new clue.

Old man: Three down, the number of times we pray each day. Ahh that's easy, F, I, V, E, right! Next, Muslims must do this once in a lifetime? Hajj of course. Ha ha, not bad for my age.

Hamid: Oh come off it, that's a kid's comic, even Hosro's too old for it now!

Old man: Rubbish, this is not a kid's comic!

Hamid: Then why's it called The Islamic Playground? And why does it have Islamic colouring activities and Islamic number puzzles?

Old man: I have never coloured in the pictures, and do not pooh-hooh the crosswords, guess this if you can! Where is the kaabah located?

Hamid: Mecca!

Old man: No, fool, it's Makkah! Not Mecca, and you want to know why? I'll tell you, tsk tsk. Due to the increasing misuse of our holy city's name, as in Motor-Mecca, Mecca-Bingo and such like, Saudi Arabia has officially changed the spelling. At the mosque we are planning to protest against the chain of pornographic cinemas called Mecca-Movies.

53

Hamid: Why bother if it's now called Makkah?

Old man: You don't understand, Muslims have a duty to be vigilant against sacrilegious and blasphemous acts and anything that is disrespectful. We must be the watchdogs for the sake of Islam!

Hamid: Watchdogs? Ha ha, take Turpin with you next time you go on a protest....

Old man: How dare you? You are getting as bad as that idiot brother-in-law of yours! Did you know Abbas thinks he's a Buddhist?

Hamid: He is a Buddhist and he's become a vegetarian.

Old man: Impossible, it is not allowed. It is written 'Whoever changes his religion, kill him.'

Hamid: So you want to kill Abbas now? Ha ha....

Hamid is laughing at him. The old man is getting angry, and he slams his fist down on the table.

Old man: It is a dishonour to our family, and why not? Not I, but there are others! If they come to know, maybe we will find him stabbed to death in a dark street.

Hamid: He's not important enough for anyone to bother going after, he's a nobody from nowhere, he's safe enough.

Old man: That's what you think!

Hamid: I'm going to the corner shop to get some bread and milk. I'll take Turpin with me.

Hamid stands up and puts his breakfast things on the tray.

Old man: How many times do I have to tell you his name is not bloody Turpin, it's Cyrus! Pass me the Quran.

Hamid: What do you want that for now? I thought you were doing your crossword.

Old man: I've told you before, tsk tsk. We can interpret the text of the Quran by using numerology. You must of course seek out the right verse, the one pertaining to the matter in question. *(Points at Hamid.)* For example when your sister told me she wanted to wed Abbas, I consulted a passage about matrimony, and do you remember? From the frequency of certain words and the numbers assigned to those words, I came to know that he was the worst possible suitor.

Hamid: *(Hamid shakes his head.)* I remember you telling us fortune telling was haram.

Old man: Nonsense, numerology is a science, pass it to me, there are things I need to know.

Hamid passes him the Quran and then leaves the sitting room. The old man flicks through the pages before finding a suitable verse. He reads on, jotting down his numbers and feverishly starts adding them together.

Old man: Holy . . . Master . . . Rumi? . . . Impossible! Abbas never! Aha! *(He looks up towards the photograph of the holy sage for inspiration; he sees it upside down.)* What?

The old man jumps up and charges over to the shelf. He picks up the photograph to set it straight and sees the bottles of wine hidden behind it. He pulls them out, and then looks to the ceiling.

Old man: Thank you Allah, message received loud and clear. *(He sniffs the bottles.)* Devils! Devils! *(Mumbles, as he plonks the bottles on the dining table.)* Ahh! . . . A fool am I? Tsk.... A mule?

CORRIDOR

The old man rushes into the corridor and aims a kick at Abbas and Faruzeh's bedroom door.

Old man: *(Shouting.)* Lazy devils! It's midday, lying in bed in filth and drunken stupor.

The old man heads into his bedroom, finds his walking stick and starts hammering on their door.

Old man: PIGS . . . GET UP I TELL YOU!

The old man presses his ear to the door and listens, he shakes his head.

Old man: PAH! *(He spits at the door.)* Useless…. Waste of time trying to wake them.

With his walking stick tucked under his arm he goes into the kitchen and gets his insulin and syringe from the fridge and returns to the sitting room.

SITTING ROOM

Sitting at the table he prepares the injection, then he stands back up steadying himself with his walking stick like he's suddenly become old and frail. He goes over to the armchair and sits down. He pulls up his tunic and gives himself the shot of insulin, after he sits back and throws the empty syringe onto the floor. He clasps his stick with both hands and closes his eyes, his mouth opens slightly. He seems to be sleeping.

The clock shows a quarter past twelve and the old man doesn't move. Then there's the sound of a bedroom door opening in the corridor. Faruzeh walks cautiously into the sitting room followed by Abbas. They both look scared.

Abbas: Oh Shit…. He's still here. I thought he'd gone out.

Faruzeh: *(Whispers.)* I can't stop now, I have to meet Sepideh at mid-day. I'm already late.

Abbas: Why the hell can't he mind his own fucking business? *(Sighs.)*

Faruzeh: Shit, shit! *(Looking at the table.)* He found the wine. *(Caresses the bottles.)* You forgot the bottles the other night, you remember? When he came home early.

Abbas: Who cares? It's just an excuse to rage at us, at me.

Faruzeh: Can't you talk to him? You've got time before you leave. Just say sorry, calm him down a bit.

Abbas: No way! *(Sulking.)*

Faruzeh: I can't face coming home tonight if you haven't had it out with him first. *(She touches Abbas's*

56

arm.) It'll be worse later, best to get it over with right now. *(She puts her head on one side like a cute bird.)* Please?

Abbas: *(Abbas goes over to the old man and pokes the syringe on the floor with his foot.)* Look he's gone! Pathetic bastard. *(He leans into the old man's face.)* In the land of nod are you?

Faruzeh: Abbas, please? . . . Look I've got to go, I'll call you later. *(She turns and leaves.)*

BATHROOM

Abbas stands still, staring at himself in the mirror. He rubs his chin, running his fingertips softly over the wiry stubble that covers his double chin. He shaves at the mirror and after he splashes cold water in his eyes then rubs his face dry.

SITTING ROOM

Abbas comes back into the sitting room. He looks at the old man, then goes over to the stereo and puts on a cassette of loud Arab pop music. He bops around the sitting room dancing to the table where the wine bottles are still standing. He takes a glass from the shelf, changes his mind and takes a swig from the bottle. He starts sniggering.

He dances back in front of the old dozy man in the chair. Abbas spins on the spot like a mad dervish, every time he faces the old man he claps his hands like a gun shot right in his face, then he spins around and around, clapping and grinning. He spins fast and he spins slow, he shimmies his arse in the old mans face, he claps his fat red hands under the old man's nose. On and on his feet stamping the floor, wooden flip-flops thumping, his hands smarting from the stinging claps. He spins onwards, kicking out his legs, his palms whizzing near the old man's face, faster and faster, he slaps his thighs, slap, slap, slap. The music slows and he dances back to the table, shoving the bottle in his mouth, letting the wine burn his guts and set him on fire. He dances back to the old man and stands in front of him, swigging on the bottle in small sips. He spills some down his chin. The wine dribbles like tears and trickles onto his white shirt. He gets angry, the childish grin spread across his fat face changes, becoming darker and sulking. He turns around and switches off the stereo. Then he steps up to the old man and stands still, stuck to the spot like a dog chained to a post.

Abbas: Hey you old bastard, wanna drink? *(He leans forward close to the old man's face.)* Go on! You cranky old fool…. Pah! *(He steps back.)* Look at you, no good for nothing, just sitting in your chair, shouting your mouth off and saying your prayers. You're ruining my life and why does my son call you Baba? I'm his bloody father! I'm sick of your bullshit, who do you think you are? . . . EH? . . . My son's father? Who am I eh? A childless donkey? Your fucking servant? *(Abbas kneels down holding the bottle out in supplication, voice whining.)* Oh Master, please I beg you, I implore you! Can I scrub your floors? Can I empty your phlegm from the glass? Can I collect your yellow toenails off the mat? Please Master? AGGH OOHH!!

The old man brings his stick sharply up between Abbas's legs, whacking him hard in the balls. Abbas staggers on his knees and reels over backward banging his head hard. He lays stunned on the carpet.

The old man sits holding his stick between his legs and stares out the window listening to Abbas throwing up. He seems bored by it all as he looks back down without expression, watching Abbas who is dazed and retching on the carpet rolled into a foetal position.

OUTSIDE FLAT

Hamid has returned on his scooter. Turpin Cyrus Babai is sitting between his legs on the floorboard. Hamid parks and enters the block of flats with the dog running at his heels.

SITTING ROOM

Abbas is now on his hands and knees, groaning as he vomits his heart and wine on the carpet. Hamid comes into the corridor singing a pop song.

Hamid: Habibi Ha Ha . . . Habibi Ha Ha . . . Habibi . . .

He walks into the sitting room, stops and looks.

An old grizzled king sits upon his throne with a mighty staff clasped in his knotted arthritic hands. His back is bowed and twisted like an old tree trunk bent by time and wind. At his feet there's a Persian garden carpet. A garden of pleasure with streams and paths, trees and beautiful borders of spring flowers, yellowed earth is worked in gold, animals and mythical creatures gather around the central pond of water. Violating this exquisite paradise is Abbas, grunting like a woman giving birth. Hamid stares hard at the old man with a look of suspicion and complicity.

Hamid: Dad? What have you done?

The old man doesn't answer. He looks away staring out the window. There is no woman giving birth in his garden, it's only his donkey son-in-law grunting on the floor face down.

Hamid: Dad, what's happened? DAD....

The old man gets up and pokes his stick at Abbas.

Old man: *(Whining like a child.)* It's his fault, not mine.... He insulted me, called me a bastard.... Look he's been drinking, in front of me! He brought alcohol into the house. I wanted to complain about this. *(He waves his stick at the table where the other bottle is.)* He wouldn't come out of his room.

Hamid: I know Faruzeh called me on the phone.

Old man: *(He reddens, realising Hamid knows.)* I fell asleep.
I'd taken my medicine. *(Points at Abbas.)* He woke me
up! Shouting at me!

The old man walks slowly out the sitting room leaning
heavily on his walking stick like an old sick man.

Hamid: DAD! *(The old man stops but he doesn't turn.)* Slow
down on the medicine . . . there are syringes all over
the house. *(The old man starts walking off.)* Dad, please
take it easy, huh? Don't be hard…. Dad?

Abbas is a pile of shiny quivering tripe, spit hangs from
his mouth and sweat runs in rivers over his pockmarked
face. His shiny eyes bloodshot and glassy spill tears like
marbles and he grunts like a pig. Hamid hauls him to his
feet, and shouldering him he drags Abbas out the door.

BATHROOM

Abbas is doubled over the toilet in silence. Hamid comes
in with the carpet. He stuffs it in the bath and runs the
shower hose to rinse the vomit off.

PATTY'S FLAT/DAY
BEDROOM

Pete is stuffing his few possessions into a plastic
shopping bag. He takes a T-shirt and some underpants
out of a drawer and chucks them in. Patty is lying on the
bed snivelling. He has hardly anything of his own to take
away from Patty's flat as he keeps everything at his mum's
house.

SITTING ROOM

Pete comes into the sitting room, scans the shelves and
takes two discs and a detective novel.

BEDROOM

Back in the bedroom he takes his photograph from the easel, then he gets his penknife out of his jeans pocket and starts to cut at the portrait painting. Patty jumps off the bed.

Patty: Ahh! No! *(She runs forward and seizes Pete's arm. He pushes her off.)* My painting!

Pete: You're not fucking showing this crap around! Telling everyone it's a portrait of me. It's my fucking portrait and I think it's shit. So I've the right. *(He throws it on the floor, grabs a corner and kicks a hole through it.)*

Patty: You Bastard! *(She's hurt and hateful.)*

The painted Pete lies on the floor all bent and twisted, his face cut, shredded and beaten. Patty can still see his crooked smile. She feels guilty, maybe she shouldn't have made his teeth so yellow. Pete kicks the canvass across the floor and strides over to the dressing table. He opens Patty's jewellery box.

Patty: What? That's my jewellery! Leave it alone. *(She runs up behind Pete. He elbows her roughly back onto the bed.)*

Pete: *(Taking earrings out the box.)* I gave you these earrings and I'm taking them back!

Patty bursts into tears. Pete has one last look round. He snatches a doll from the windowsill, yanks its head off and chucks it on the floor. He goes out into the corridor and opens the front door. Patty races after him.

STAIRCASE OUTSIDE FLAT

Pete steps out through the front door. Patty's right behind trying to pull him back inside.

Patty: Don't go, please, nothing happened…. I tell you nothing happened!

Pete: Fuck you, I saw you … I tell ya … from the bloody window, you fucking parked outside the house. *(He slaps Patty's face.)* You're lucky I don't kick your

61

fucking face in! Piss taker. Outside the fucking
window, lit up by the lamp post. Shithead I saw ya!
Pete punches her back through the door with his fist and
starts down the stairs. Patty comes after him, and he
pushes her down on the steps.

Pete: Ugly bitch! I shoulda left ya a long time ago.

The crooked man leaves the crooked house with his
crooked treasures and the crooked woman cries crooked
tears as she collapses on the stairs.

BABAI FLAT SITTING ROOM/NIGHT

The television is on. Abbas is watching the screen like an
old donkey peering out over the stable door. His milky
eyes blinded by cataracts can only see shadows in the dim
light. His ears like crazy wings, twitch, straining for
sounds. His velvet muzzle breathes the aroma of fresh
dung and hope. He can't move. He's wrapped up in
thoughts that bind him like tight leather straps cutting
through his old worn fur, deep into his flesh. This
defeated donkey man is silent. He sits, neither hoping nor
dreaming. Long ago he ran in the sun, his neck hung with
garlands. Pom poms and silk tassels bobbed and bounced
around his head as he galloped through the dust. His
reigns were decorated with embroidered flowers and
scented with tiny orange pomander balls.

Hosro is playing a video game. Faruzeh has fallen asleep
on the sofa. The old man is reciting verses of the Quran
over the sound of the television. Hamid is dialing a
telephone number, it rings but no one answers. The old
man's voice keeps droning.

JAMSHID'S FLAT/NIGHT
SITTING ROOM

Zina's standing in the corner ironing next to a huge pile
of wrinkled clothes. Jamshid and his father are watching
the television and his mother is parked at the abandoned

dining table. Salim, their eldest son strolls in; Jamshid
looks at his watch and Salim plonks himself down on the
sofa.

Salim: All right Dad? Good film is it?

Jamshid: Not bad…. Why so late? Where you been?

Salim: Peshman's…. I'm starving hungry…. *(He keeps
watching the television.)* MUM . . . what's for dinner?

Zina: We already eating before.

Jamshid: *(Without turning his head.)* ZINA . . . get Salim
some food!

Zina puts down the iron with a scowl and goes to the
kitchen. After a while she returns.

Zina: Dinner ready. *(Salim saunters over to the table, and she
puts a large vegetable omelette down in front of him and pushes
a breadbasket across the table. Salim looks down at his plate.)*

Salim: I don't want this! I fancy some fried chicken and
chips.

Zina: This what I cooking tonight.

Jamshid: *(Without turning his head.)* Go on, get the boy
some chicken…. He's hungry, a growing lad no?

Zina goes out to the kitchen taking the omelette with her.
Salim watches the TV from the dining table. Finally Zina
returns. She bangs a huge plate of fried chicken legs down
on the table in front of him. Salim starts to tuck in and
Zina returns to her ironing. Then Salim notices his
Grandma for the first time.

Salim: Do I have to eat with her here in front of me?
Can't you take her to her bedroom?

Zina: Can't, I iron shirts now, after clean table, after
Maman go bed….

Salim: She's dribbled food all down her front, why don't
you clean her up?

Jamshid: What's that? *(He half raises himself from his
armchair turning to look first at his mother then at his wife.)*
ZINA look she's wetting herself! There's a puddle of

63

urine under her wheelchair. What's wrong with you?
Can you not show my mother some respect?
Salim stands up with his plate and gives his grandmother
and the puddle a wide berth. He sits down on the sofa
and carries on eating while he watches the television. Zina
fetches a mop and bucket full of soapsuds. She's wearing
a pair of rubber gloves and begins mopping the floor
under the wheelchair, squeezing out the mop into the
bucket. When she's finished with the floor, Zina wheels
the grandma out the door.

GRANDMA'S BEDROOM
Zina picks up the tiny old dwarf doll and throws her on a
dusty rosewood commode chair. She weighs nothing. The
old dwarf grips the arm rests to stop herself from being
blown out the window and away into the sky. She clings
to life and won't let go; her hands are like claws encrusted
with gold rings and sparkling jewels. In her bedchamber
there's a table covered with silver and gilt framed
photographs, memories from the golden days. Once the
old doll had been a maid to the Empress Farah's cousin
and she'd been rewarded with a hoard of jewels given to
her by the princess Sohrab. Zina adores her mother-in-
law's booty and seethes with envy, but she'll have to wait
till the old dwarf dies before they'll belong to her. On
black days she ties the dwarf doll to the commode with
an old stocking and wears the rings and necklaces herself.
And if the dwarf should mouth incoherent growls at her
she'll shove a sock in her mouth. Zina cackles and doesn't
give a damn as she turns round and round like a ballerina
in a music box; she waves her hand languidly at the
speckled mirror, blowing kisses to her reflection while her
fingers sparkle and flutter with diamonds and sapphires.
She wants to wear them now while she is still young and
moist; she hates this tiny shrivelled dwarf doll, with her

hairy face moles, showing her what in old age she will become.

PATTY'S FLAT KITCHEN/NIGHT

Patty is in her kitchen. She's wearing a bright red Kimono with a dragon embroidered on the back. Her hair is scraped back and her eyes are red and puffy. She's sitting at the kitchen table, and her friend Melanie is standing at the sink wearing a silver leatherette motorbike jacket, skin-tight jeans and silver platform sandals. Melanie's eyes are made up in the Egyptian style and her hair is cropped short and dyed platinum; she has a pierced nose and lip. The table is covered in beer bottles and ashtrays overflowing with fag butts. There's a doll sitting propped up against a coffee mug, its head on the table. The sink behind Melanie is piled dangerously high with dirty saucepans, frying pans and plates.

Melanie: *(Waving her fag at Patty.)* You wait and see…. He'll come back they always do.

Patty: He won't.

Melanie: He will, he'll get over it, he's mad with jealousy. *(She puffs on her fag.)* When he realises that it's all over nothing, that there's nothing between you and this Hamid, he can't blame you, if some bloke tries it on….

Patty: He saw us from the window.

Melanie: So what? Nothing happened right?

Patty shrugs and sips her beer; she leans back in her chair and holds her bottle up as though it were a microphone.

Patty: Well . . . he's . . . he's sort of sexy. *(She grins to herself.)* He's a bit fat, but I like him and I can't help it, if I didn't I'd have got straight out the car.

Melanie's eyes widen, she loosens the crutch of her jeans and sits down in front of Patty.

Melanie: Do you mean to say Pete saw you screwing in the car with Hamid? *(Patty nods.)* Well! He won't come

65

back then; you've hurt his pride. I know Pete! He'll never live it down.

Patty: I know.

Melanie: So, It's your own bloody fault.

Patty: I've been with Pete eight years . . . I know he lives with his mum, but he was always here. We were getting really close to him moving in with me . . . I'll miss him . . . so much.

Melanie: And this Hamid, what about him?

Patty: Oh, I don't know, I like him but....

Melanie starts yawning and Patty gets up and goes to the window. She looks at her reflection, holding the curtain under her eyes in a parody of a veiled woman. She stares hard at herself.

Patty: He might make me wear a veil over my head. *(She pulls the curtain up over her head covering her face, Melanie cackles.)*

BABAI FLAT/DAY
CORRIDOR

The muezzin music is blaring out at full volume, and the old man is kicking viciously at Abbas and Faruzeh's bedroom door. He hammers with his walking stick, cracking the paint while Hosro tries to pull him away.

Hosro: Baba, Baba please, don't.

The old man elbows him away still kicking hard at the door.

Old man: Not even to atone for your sins.... After what you did! Curse the day I let you under my roof! PIG! Pray now or be DAMNED!

The door suddenly bursts open. The old man stumbles against the doorway as Abbas in his underpants and socks charges through into the corridor. He butts the old man hard against the wall and races into the sitting room; the old man rushes after him.

Old man: YOU BASTARD!

SITTING ROOM

As Abbas runs in, he skids on the prayer mat and catches hold of the sofa to stop himself crashing. The old man comes galloping up behind and throws himself on Abbas's back. His knotted arms grow longer and harder, locking around his neck, choking the air out of him. Hosro who's followed them into the room turns and runs back into the corridor.

Hosro: MUM, MUM, QUICK!

Abbas tries to pry himself free; he can only see stars as he gasps for air. Then he sinks his huge yellow bucked teeth into the old man's papery flesh, and the metallic salty taste of blood seeps into his mouth.

Old man: Rabid dog! You Bastard, you bit me!

The old man lets go and seizes Abbas by his ponytail. Abbas and the old man wrestle each other. The old man clings to his vest and Abbas elbows him in the gut. The old man collapses winded on the floor.

Abbas runs to the table, grabs the Ghetto Blaster and hurls it at the window. It only cracks the glass and thuds to the floor, still calling him to prayer, mocking his rage and power. He picks it up again; his face is as red as a donkey's arse. He runs at the window screaming louder than the muezzin chanting, throwing it with all his might, it smashes the glass yet falls down on the floor again. Abbas will never give up; at last, finally, wonderfully, he shoves it through the broken windowpane, cutting his hands and arms.

Faruzeh and Hosro have come into the room. They are staring at Abbas. He stands there with shining eyes; once and for all he has thrown the muezzin music out the window. His man breasts glisten with sweat, he drips blood on the carpet, he's wild, he's fat and he's triumphant beyond any doubt. He can feel his tiny angel wings as sharp as shoulder blades pushing through his skin. The old man has got up and is making his way out the room, stumbling and winded.

Old man: You saw him! You saw what he did! *(Pointing wildly at Abbas.)*

Hosro: Dad, You're dripping blood. I'll help you; let's go to the bathroom.

Abbas is just standing there dazed. He lets Hosro take his arm like a dumb brain battered boxer.

OUTSIDE PATTY'S FLAT/DAY

The street traffic is moving slowly like a stagnant river. The people don't seem real it's too early in the day. They stare out from the car windows like cut-out paper men. A man stands outside a door ringing a bell; he has a bouquet of wrapped flowers. The door opens and Patty steps onto the street, she reaches out, breathing in the sweet fragrance. People stare at the woman as she spins the bouquet rich with colours and scents around and around making a kaleidoscope, like a pinwheel firework in the wind set on fire, turning and burning. She finds a card and reads it, and then she gathers the flowers in her arms like a baby and goes back inside.

OUTSIDE SHOP/DAY

Outside on the street an old motorbike goes by. Through the shop window Hamid is seated at the counter reading a newspaper. He picks up the shop phone, listens, says something and replaces the phone. He then snatches up his keys and jacket and leaves the shop pulling down the shutters.

DANCE CLASS/NIGHT

Patty walks into the dance class. She has dressed and simpered in front of her mirror practising this moment all day long, but Hamid is not there. Amina is dancing with the other students and she waves to Patty. As the music finishes Patty walks over to her.

Amina: Hi, how are you?

Patty: Fine thanks, I'm a bit late, Hamid's not here yet?

Amina: Oh he can't come tonight. *(Patty looks expectantly at her as the music starts up again.)* He phoned earlier. *(Amina twirls.)* Family problems. *(Amina snaps her fingers in front of Patty's eyes.)* Don't worry. *(Shimmies.)* Come on. *(She holds out her hand to Patty.)* Figure of eight in one line….

The women line up following Amina. They begin swaying their hips moving forwards then sideways. They dance winking at each other, shaking their breasts.

BABAI FLAT/NIGHT
OLD MAN'S BEDROOM

The old man is in bed; he's blowing his nose and wiping his eyes. There's a tray on the bed with a bowl of rice, and Hamid is sitting on the edge of the bed with a spoonful suspended in mid air.

Hamid: Come on Dad! Just one, you've had nothing all day . . . think about your insulin levels. DAD, if you don't eat I'll call the Doctor! Then you'll be taken to hospital! DO YOU WANT THAT?

Old man: At least I'll be out from under your feet!

Hamid: Please Dad, just try to eat.

Old man: No one remembers your Mother!

Hamid: WHAT! Of course they do.

Old man: Because it seems like everyone has forgotten her, except for myself.

Hamid: Dad, don't say that, I remember Maman . . . we all do.

Old man: Sometimes I feel I'd be better off dead! I'm just a rotting carcass, despised under my own roof.

Hamid: DAD!

Old man: Just go away right now. I want to be alone . . .
to remember your mother.

The old man rolls over turning away. Hamid looks at him
lying there, then he notices the spoon in his hand and the
bowl of food on the tray. He eats a mouthful, then
another and begins tucking in. The old man springs up.

Old man: Look at you! Even you've turned your back on
me, taking the bread from my mouth. There's no end
to your greed! *(He snatches the spoon and dish from
Hamid.)* You've nearly eaten it all!

Hamid: Well you didn't want it! I'm hungry . . . I've had
nothing since early morning.

Old man: FOOD! All you think of is your gut, not your
soul . . . go away! And take your greed with you, I
want to be alone!

The old man turns his back again, throwing the dish and
spoon on the tray. Hamid looks at him. He seems even
thinner under the worn flannel sheets, like a broken ship
mast, fallen on the deck and buried in ragged sails.
Hamid reaches out and pats the old man's sharp bony
shoulder then stands up.

Old man: Wait! *(He sits back up.)* Help me to get up, I'm
going into the sitting room and I need Hosro. I want
to surf the web!

Hamid: Not again Dad, last time you bought that
chandelier. . . .

Old man: So what! Has the ceiling fallen down? Shut up
and just turn on the computer for me. *(He hits away
Hamid's helping hand.)* I can get myself out of bed!

Hamid: What do you want to buy this time?

Old man: None of your bloody business, it's a surprise.

Hamid: For me?

Old man: No, you can do your own shopping and buy
your own surprises.

Hamid: Something for Abbas? To make peace. . . .

Old man: For that Donkey? Never! Now stop sticking your nose in, and call Hosro on the cellular, tell him I need him home right now!

SITTING ROOM
(Later on.) Hosro and the old man are sitting at the dining table looking at Internet web shops.

Old man: No, no, those won't do, tsk! Something more, well, higher off the floor and protected from drafts.... Did you know his feet are always cold?

Hosro: How could I know? How do you know?

Old Man: Don't be a smart arse! We all know he offers his paw to shake.

Hosro: Yeah he's so clever! *(He giggles.)* Baba, you shook his paw?

Old man: I might have done, just once, or twice! Ahh! *(He peers through his spectacles at the screen.)* Now that's more like it, that one. *(He jabs his finger.)*

Hosro: Are you sure Baba?

Old man: Yes, it's the best one! If you're going to do something, do it properly, that's what I say.

Hosro: Why can't he sleep on my bed?

Old man: No he can't! . . . Next you'll have me buying him a miniature bed with silk sheets....

Hosro: They probably only sell them in America!

Old man: You never know, let's go and look.

Hosro types in 'Luxury dog bed.'

STREET OUTSIDE BABAI FLAT/DAY
It's early morning; the loud hooting and roaring of cars and motorbikes fills the air.
The Babai's flat still has the curtains drawn. No muezzin music comes blasting out the windows this morning.

INSIDE DOLL FACTORY/DAY

Patty is in the packing room sitting with four other women at a long table; they are surrounded by cardboard boxes. The boxes are full of polystyrene chips with dolls heads and arms poking out like cadaverous potted plants. There are shelves full of dolls, with frozen smiles inside transparent plastic bags. Their breasts are pointed like cones without nipples; they're long-limbed and have no pubic hair and no vaginas, just a mass of yellow gold hair sprouting from their heads. Patty and the other women are fitting the dolls together, putting heads and limbs onto the doll's torsos. Patty has a pile of limbless 'Drink and Wet' dolls. She checks the hole in the mouth by inserting a mini water bottle and squeezing, then she holds the doll over a bucket to empty the water out the small hole in its bottom.

Patty: Jesus! These are really low tech, they only wet
    while they're drinking, and they can't hold their pee.

A secretary sits at a large reception desk on a chrome swivel chair by the door. She's wearing heavy makeup and her hair has been blow dried into huge wings on either side of her face.

Patty tries to call Hamid on her mobile phone. The secretary gets up and lifts a smart beauty case out from under the desk and walks past the women.

Woman one: Oy! Wake up Patty. *(She nudges Patty as the secretary marches past them to the bathroom, banging the door hard behind her.)*

Woman two: Gonna go and give the boss his blowjob, darling? *(To the slamming door.)*

Woman one: Shit a brick, PATTY! You've gone and put the legs in the armholes!

Patty's still fiddling with her telephone. She looks at the doll, confused by its appearance.

Patty: I don't feel well, I think I've got the flue; I'd better go home. *(Patty puts her phone in her bag and puts her jacket on.)*

Woman one: They'll dock it off your wages!

Patty: I think I'm gonna be sick, I gotta go.

Woman two: At least body bag that lot before you skive off!

Patty looks doubtfully at the pile of dolls and reluctantly starts pushing them into polythene bags. She pulls the bags tightly over their faces, and plants them up to their waists in the polystyrene filled boxes.

INSIDE SHOP/DAY

Faruzeh is sitting at the counter going through a pile of invoices with her calculator. Patty comes in and walks straight over to her.

Patty: Excuse me, I'm looking for Hamid.

Faruzeh looks up, trying to work out what Patty could want with her brother.

Faruzeh: *(A bit suspicious.)* I'm afraid he's not in today. *(She waits to see what Patty will say.)*

Patty: Look! I really need to see him. I've taken the day off work to find him…. I've tried calling a dozen times. *(Desperate.)*

Faruzeh: *(Feeling sorry for her.)* He's at home, our father hasn't been well, he'll be back at work in a few days.

Patty: Is he at home now?

Faruzeh: *(Cagey.)* He was when I left.

Patty: Please, could I just call him? Could you give me his home number?

Faruzeh: Well…. *(Undecided.)* All right, but please if our father answers, just say you have the wrong number. He gets a bit upset sometimes, he's very old you know.

Faruzeh looks at Patty, trying to judge how far she can trust her, and then she writes the number on a notepad and tears it off slowly. She slides it across the counter in a secretive way.

BABAI FLAT CORRIDOR/DAY

The phone is ringing in the corridor. Hamid comes through from the sitting room with bare feet. Before he can reach for the phone he treads on a syringe that the old man chucked away. He stumbles against the bicycles and the phone stops ringing. Hamid picks up the syringe and heads into his father's bedroom. He can see him through the doorway, sitting up in bed, reading and mechanically feeding himself sweets from a tin. Every now and then he tosses one to Turpin Cyrus Babai who is sitting on the end of his bed.

Hamid: Dad you'll make the dog fat! He's beginning to look like a baby pig....

Old man: Shut up! What do you know? Here you are Cyrus. *(He tosses him another fudge cube.)*

PATTY'S FLAT/DAY
KITCHEN

The kitchen is a mess. There are plates piled high in the sink, beer cans and bottles on the table and Patty's two cats are eating up on the worktop. Patty holds the telephone receiver to her ear; it's ringing faintly, while Melanie goes through the telephone directory and finds Behdad Babai. She checks it's the same number on the scrap of paper Faruzeh gave Patty.

Melanie: Yeah, it's the right number, try again later....

Patty puts the phone back on the hook.

BEDROOM

Patty rummages in her chest of drawers. She pulls out a child's plastic charm bracelet hung with miniature figurines inspired by 'Harry Potter'. She holds them in the palm of her hand under the light.

Melanie: What are you doin with them?

Patty: Long story, it's a present for Hamid.

Melanie: Miniature plastic dolls?

Patty: His Grandma put dolls in the hubbly bubbly, he hasn't got any himself, so I'm giving him some.

Melanie: He'll think you're weird, off your rocker, lost the plot!

Patty: No he won't, I need a nice box to put them in, he sent me a bouquet of flowers.

Melanie: So?

Patty: You wouldn't understand! I have to see him, I'm gonna go to his house and wait for him to get back. *(She empties a velvet box full of earrings and puts the miniature doll bracelet inside, then takes her crash helmet and keys from the bed.)* I've gotta go now, you can let yourself out!

OUTSIDE BABAI FLAT/DAY

(Early afternoon.) Hamid is getting into his car; he's wearing a T-shirt, jeans, white socks and sandals. He puts a small portable cassette player and a large sports bag on the back seat, and then starts the engine.

Patty is coming along the road on her moped, as she gets closer she waves to Hamid but he doesn't see her. He pulls out onto the road two cars in front of Patty, and then drives off down the street with her following him. Hamid drives along listening to loud Persian Santur music. He turns into a leafy residential street and pulls over to the side of the road and stops.

JAMSHID'S FLAT BEDROOM /DAY

The flat is on the ground floor. Zina's in the bedroom standing next to the window. She's looking into a compact mirror, drawing kohl slowly around her eyes. There's a double bed, a trouser press, two chairs and a dressing table with a dictionary and exercise book open on top. In the corner of the room is a stack of boxes filled with electric toasters.

The sound of a car comes through the open window. Zina snaps her compact shut and leans to look out the window on to the street. She then steps back and pulls down the blinds to darken the already dingy room.

ROAD OUTSIDE JAMSHID'S FLAT/DAY

Patty parks her moped on the other side of the road. She looks over to Hamid in his car, now she's embarrassed and unsure if she did the right thing by following him. Hamid is leaning over the back seat; he pulls a pair of white gloves out of his bag and puts them on. The music is still playing loudly as Patty decides to just go and give him the dolls. She knows he'll understand, and she hurries towards Hamid's car.

Hamid pulls a burqa out of the bag; he sits back round and pulls it over his head first. Patty stands stock-still at the back window of his car looking in.

Hamid gets out carrying the bag and the cassette player. He can't see properly with the burqa on as it has a mesh screen that covers his eyes. He misses putting the key in the car door several times until he puts his face very close to the lock, and he can't see Patty who's standing like a ghost, frozen to the spot and speechless.

With his new found tunnel vision he fumbles the keys into his bag and goes up the front path to Jamshid's building. He rings the bell and disappears through the main door into the hall. The front door shuts with a clunk. Patty squeezes up her eyes like she's peering through thick smoke, frowning, unable to understand. She looks at her watch, lights a cigarette and goes to sit on a low wall on the opposite side of the road.

JAMSHID'S FLAT/DAY
BEDROOM
Hamid puts the cassette player down on the dressing
table and fiddles with the rewind and forward buttons.

Hamid: *(Falsetto.)* Have you memorised your exercises
Zina?

Zina: Yes, of course.

Hamid: *(Falsetto.)* Good girl, you're making wonderful
progress! *(He pats her bottom.)*

Zina sits down on the bed watching him. He presses play
on the cassette player. The tape plays a loud and un-
interesting English lesson in Hamid's falsetto voice.
'I AM WALKING, I WAS WALKING, ARE YOU
WALKING? WALK WITH ME. I AM SLEEPING, I
WAS SLEEPING, ARE YOU SLEEPING? SLEEP
WITH ME….'

SITTING ROOM
The English lesson filters softly out under the bedroom
door into the sitting room. Jamshid creeps over with a
glass and presses it against the wall to listen in. After a
while he stops and crosses the sitting room going into the
kitchen while the tape plays on.

BEDROOM
Hamid lifts off his veil and lifts up his burqa, underneath
he's wearing black silk boxer shorts. With his skirts up he
sits down on the chair and Zina straddles him. Hamid
and Zina start snogging.

SITTING ROOM
Jamshid returns to the sitting room with a drink. He sits
on the sofa, kicks off his pointed Moroccan slippers and
puts his feet up. He flicks through the television channels
with his remote control, holding his drink on his stomach

while from the bedroom comes the distinct sound of
Zina's lesson.

'IF I WERE RICH I'D BUY A PALACE, IF I WERE
STRONG I'D HELP YOU LIFT YOUR SUITCASE,
IF I WEREN'T RICH I COULDN'T BUY A PALACE,
IF I WEREN'T STRONG I COULDN'T LIFT YOUR
SUITCASE....'

Jamshid settles on a western film; he takes a sip from his
drink then rests the glass on the coffee table and lights
himself a cigarette.

BEDROOM
Zina unbuttons her blouse and Hamid dives inside with
his hands. She's sitting astride him, wearing a pair of black
zip boots and her red skirt is rucked up round her thighs.
She bounces energetically up and down in Hamid's lap
while he has his face passionately buried inside her
blouse.

SITTING ROOM
Jamshid gets up and looks towards the bedroom door,
then he wanders out to the kitchen returning with a
packet of crisps. He puts his feet up again and feeds
himself mechanically while watching the television. He
drinks and burps, picks his nose and scratches his arse.

OUTSIDE JAMSHID'S FLAT/DAY
The front door of Jamshid's building opens and a woman
with a pram comes out. Patty jumps up, the woman looks
suspiciously at her and wheels off down the street. Patty
relaxes when she sees it's not Hamid, but as the woman
disappears round the corner she crosses over the road
and stands at the gate. She takes the little velvet box from
her jacket pocket and opens it, staring at the miniature
wizard dolls. Imbibing herself with their magical powers
she goes to the front door to look at the names on the

doorbells. They're all English names except for Mohamed Jamshid. She takes a deep breath and rings the bell then expels her breath and waits. Though right now she can't wait any longer; she's waited all she can, she's phoned him a hundred times, she's followed him half way across town and now she's mad to see him.

Jamshid comes to the door, he frowns when he sees Patty; he thinks she wants to sell him something.

Patty: Sorry to bother you but….

Jamshid: *(Interrupting her.)* NO! We don't want to buy anything, thank you. *(He starts to shut the door.)*

Patty: *(Trying to see beyond him into the corridor.)* I need to speak with Hamid. It won't take a moment, could you ask him to come to the door. My names Patty, Patty Mcluskey.

Jamshid: *(Frowning and irritated.)* No one of that name here! My sons are not at home; they are at the school and name's not Hamid…. Someone is playing big joke on you or maybe you are foolish woman! *(He smiles sarcastically; he shakes his head and starts to shut the door.)*

Patty: NO Wait! I saw him go inside half an hour ago!

Jamshid: Not into my house he didn't. That's enough!

Patty: I know it was him he had a black veil thing on. He must have come to your house he was wearing Muslim clothes!

Jamshid's face whitens as he listens. It dawns on him and he realises what's going on in the bedroom. His mouth gapes open, his eyes bulge and he bangs the door shut in Patty's face.

In the wind of the slamming door she breathes in the scent of cardamons and boiled cabbage, then she hears a loud scream from the window on the corner.

JAMSHID'S FLAT BEDROOM/DAY

Jamshid storms into the bedroom. The English lesson tape is still playing. Zina near to climax is bouncing feverishly up and down, still sitting astride Hamid.

Jamshid: YOU FILTHY BITCH!

Zina jumps up pulling her skirt down and holding her blouse together, screaming like a baby. Jamshid slaps Zina around the face. She screams louder and throws herself down on the bed.

Zina: He make me do it…. I no want him…. *(Burying her face in her hands.)*

Jamshid: SHUT YOUR MOUTH!

Jamshid grabs a coat hanger from the trouser press. He leaps forward and whacks Hamid about the head and shoulders.

Jamshid: SON OF A DOG! PIMP! *(Hamid struggles to his feet. Jamshid brings the coat hanger down. He misses Hamid and hits the chair back. The coat hanger cracks and splinters.)* MY DICK ON YOUR FOREHEAD! MY SHIT BETWEEN YOUR TEETH!

He plunges the spike end of the hanger into Hamid's fatty chest. It cuts through the skin and red blood spills out, first like a shiny red poppy, then turning dark and welling up, seeping down his guts. Jamshid goes to stab him again but Hamid pulls the burqa down around him and turns fast for the window. He stumbles and skids in his white socks across the bedroom, ducking as Jamshid slashes at him, ripping the burqa from behind.

Zina screeches like a mad peacock. Jamshid turns, seizes her by the hair and punches her in the face. Meanwhile Hamid's half way through the window as Zina crawls to the top of the bed on her hands and knees, blood and snot running out her nose. Jamshid picks up Hamid's sandals.

Jamshid: I SHIT ON YOUR FATHER'S GRAVE! I PISS ON YOUR HEAD! *(Hamid jumps out the window* *in his burqa and socks; Jamshid throws Hamid's sandals at his retreating back.)* YOU SON OF A SHOE!

The English lesson is still playing.

'IF I WERE A DOG I'D BRING YOUR SHOES, IF I WERE A CAT I'D CLIMB A TREE....'

Jamshid picks up the cassette player and hurls it at the wall.

OUTSIDE JAMSHID'S FLAT/DAY

Patty is standing on the path outside the front door listening to the screaming and shouting coming from the ground floor window. The shutters suddenly open and Hamid appears; he has a bruised eye and cut face. In his socks and burqa he jumps out the window and lands heavily on his knees. He gets up rubbing the grit from his battered legs and runs out into the street. He hasn't even noticed Patty and she runs after him.

Hamid stops at his car, realises he has no key and tries the door handle. Patty has arrived next to him. Jamshid comes out of the building and starts marching towards them.

Hamid: SHIT!!

Patty: *(Patty touches Hamid's arm.)* Get on my moped, come on, run!

Hamid suddenly realises Patty is there beside him. She's appeared from nowhere like a god damn angel and the sun is breaking through the clouds. She stands in her shining armour and everything else dims and fades away. She'll spirit him away upon her trusted moped. She doesn't know why he jumped from the window with a burqa round his neck nor why the man is chasing him, she doesn't care either.

Patty and Hamid leg it over the street; Patty pulls on her crash helmet, Hamid hitches up his skirt and climbs on the back of the moped, and they screech off wobbling down the road.

Jamshid stares after them and then he looks along the street. There are at least five neighbours staring out their windows at him. He hangs his head and goes back into his house.

PATTY'S FLAT BATHROOM/DAY
(Late afternoon.) The bathroom is dark and seamy; there are candles and incense burning around the bathtub and basin mirror. Hamid and Patty are in the bath. It's an old iron tub with lion claw feet standing in the middle of the room.

On the floor there's a washing up bowl full of ice cubes, and placed next to the bathtub a stool with a bottle of whisky, cigarettes and an ashtray.

Hamid's holding a flannel with ice cubes over his black eye. He takes a swig from the bottle, rattling the wizard doll charm bracelet he's wearing. Patty is lying back with her legs split apart hanging over the sides of the bath. She's smoking a cigarette, blowing smoke into the hot steaming air.

Patty: I'm gonna paint you…. I'm gonna paint you jumping out the window, with that fucking veil round your neck and your black eye.

Hamid: *(He smiles.)* Thanks!

Patty: And then I'm gonna paint you with a great big dick, a hard on, stickin outer your trousers, sitting on a throne, and a herd of women all in a line like cows, queuing up for you, bringing you gifts like the three kings for Jesus.

Hamid lets the flannel slip into the water and kisses her leg. Patty takes the bottle from him. Her puckered pouty lips clamp round the bottleneck and she tips the whisky down her throat. Her guts burn and hot snakes wriggle around inside of her making her feel hot and slippery.

Patty: You are fucking mad!

Hamid: *(He smiles.)* Yeah.

BABAI FLAT/DAY
SITTING ROOM
(Late afternoon.) The old man is sitting in his chair
wearing a long white grubby tunic. He's reading a
newspaper and Hosro is studying his physics homework
at the dining table. Underneath his school book Hosro
has a pornographic magazine; he lets the pages of his
textbook fall and cover it whenever the old man looks up.

Hosro: Baba, Can I use your calculator?

Old man: Getting stuck? Huh! You have to learn to
 concentrate on numbers, see here!

The old man strides on his bandy legs across to the book
shelf, trying to walk low and stay hidden, his legs bent, his
back bent, his head hung down, he creeps along hiding
from snipers that only he can see.

Old man: Give me a number, any number! What's the
 root? Ha, I can tell you without a calculator.

He makes his way towards Hosro, who covers over his
porno magazine. He gets a huge calculator down from the
shelf and slides it across the table then he shifts stiffly
back to his chair.

Old man: If your names on the wrong number . . . umm?
 You can make it into number five, and that'll cut off
 all these bad workings . . . and you'll get something
 someway.

Hosro: How? *(He smiles at the old man, he already knows.)*

Old man: If your name is not agreed with you, you can
 have the name in number three. It will work for your
 prosperous.... And this is a very deep story, you have
 to watch when you change your name.... You have to
 write it a hundred thousand times! Tsk! A hundred
 thousand times. Now back at home we had a
 neighbour, she was a widow and only had one son,
 and he was a fine boy, you know? Very tall, very
 honest and hardworking. Then came the time for him
 to marry and his mother chose him a wife. All the

astrology was perfect, PERFECT! But it was no use at all, this girl . . . she was nasty to the mother, wasted her husbands money down the toilet on perfumes and jewellery, and would not keep house because she was divooneh . . . crazy! *(He taps the side of his head.)* All day at the cinema, no laundry, no cooking, nothing! So of course he divorced her! Then after a year he married again, and this time his mother gave much money to the astrologists to get it right. They looked for a wife who would be diligent in the kitchen and you know what?

Hosro: *(Shakes his head.)* What?

Old man: This girl burnt down the kitchen and argued like the devil with everyone. She had a sharp tongue, better she had been born a dumb mule, and so he divorced again. Then at last I said to the widow, 'We must change your son's name, there is nothing else to be done.' So after much calculation he was named Hooman, I gave him some exercise books, and he wrote his new name a hundred thousand times. I told his mother, 'Now you must find a girl by the name of Kobra, no other name will do.' It was all in the numbers you see? And you know what?

Hosro: *(Shrugs.)* What?

Old man: He married a fat beautiful girl named Kobra and she was kind to his mother and generous with beggars, most of all she gave him nine children! Think of that, nine! Now nine is a very auspicious number too. . . .

The doorbell rings. The old man gets up and shuffles out the doorway. Hosro hunches over his books as the old man passes then he puts his magazine inside his textbook. He can hear the old man in the corridor.

Old Man: Bring it right up! At last! *(Shouts to Hosro.)* The furniture has arrived!

Hosro helps to carry a tiny settee through to the sitting room. They rip off the plastic cover, and then he and the old man push the furniture around putting the settee next to the old man's armchair.

Old man: Now Cyrus! Come on! Up!

Turpin Cyrus Babai follows orders and jumps onto his own miniature faux black leather settee with leopard print cushions.

Hosro: Look there's room for me too!

Hosro sits down next to the dog and the old man plonks himself down in the armchair.

Old man: Do you know I saw a film on the telly once, about an old rich woman who had one of those sausage dogs. Guess what? It slept in a miniature four-poster bed. Ridiculous woman, what a fool! Hah hah!

Hosro: *(Giggles.)* Really Baba?

Old man: I remember it had curtains for privacy.

They sit in silence, smiling and saying nothing, they don't need to. Suddenly the doorbell rings again.

Old man: Tsk, what have those delivery fools forgotten now? *(He goes back out into the hall.)*

After a few minutes, the old man walks back into the sitting room followed by Jamshid.

Jamshid: I want to talk in private! *(Looking at Hosro.)*

Old man: Hosro take your work to your room and take Cyrus too.

Jamshid waits, looking disgusted as Hosro passes by him with the dog in his arms.

Old man: Why have you come here? As you can see he's not at home, he's at the shop!

Jamshid: NO! He is not at your shop. You have no idea what he's up to! Did you know he has big advertisement poster in the shop window? For a widow who is giving private lessons to Muslim housewives!

Old man: So what?

Jamshid: Only there is no widow, he's the widow disguised in a burqa! *(Jamshid pauses, waiting for the old man's comprehension and outrage.)*

Old man: Nonsense!

Jamshid: *(Furious.)* It is true! He came…. *(Louder.)* He has been coming many weeks to MY house, for giving English lessons to MY wife! This widow is telling everyone she only giving lesson in private room. *(He shakes his head wildly, his wiry beard glistening with sprayed saliva.)* I AM BELIEVING HE IS A WOMAN! I AM SENDING HIM TO MY BEDROOM ALONE WITH MY WIFE! *(He slaps his forehead.)* Just think with my poor mother there! Who knows what scenes she has witnessed? The shame! He has defiled my home, dishonoured me…. *(His voice rises higher, screeching.)* IT IS WORSE THAN DEATH! *(He freezes, his jaw drops open, then he hisses choking and spitting.)* He tricked money from me, I paid him!

Old man: *(Confused, backing away.)* Paid him?

Jamshid: For the lessons…. Do you not understand? We are all believing he is harmless old widow!…. *(The old man sits down shocked on the dog's settee.)* I know of other men in our community who have paid him for same set up! AND NOW! IN THE END! I DISCOVER THE DEVIL IN MY BEDROOM! *(He shakes his head, his lips twisted in a sick smile.)* He ran away but I will find him! I will ruin him and your family, all of you! Who do you think will be coming to your shop after this? . . . Also much divorce! All will want him dead!

There is silence as they stare at each other. Time stands still while the old man's mind is working.

Old man: *(He looks right into Jamshid's eyes with a piercing gaze.)* What about your honour? Your son's honour? It is also bad for you if this becomes public.

86

Jamshid: *(His eyes narrow.)* I want punishment! Something must be done! *(Voice rising.)* Do you think I can sit and do nothing?

Old man: What do you want to do?

Jamshid: Sharia! *(His eyes shine with visions.)*

Old man: *(Whispers.)* Sharia? Here?

Jamshid: We can organize in some back garden and justice will be done!

Old man: *(Shouting.)* Are you mad? We are here! This is the land of Kafirs! We cannot carry on as if we were back at home. *(Throwing his hands up in despair.)* Just look at the telly! *(Jabs his finger at the television; Jamshid spins round staring at the black screen.)* Men and women having affairs all over the place, in cars and offices and even in bloody toilets! And what are the consequences? I'll tell you! *(Stands up, stepping towards Jamshid.)* Nothing! Bloody nothing, no one has to pay, they do it, and that's the end of it!

Jamshid: *(Whining.)* There must be justice!

Old man: Justice? Hah! What is justice? What can I do? I can shout at him till I break his ears, I can beat him when I catch him asleep; otherwise he's too fast for my stick.... And that's it! That's the most I can do, and even that's illegal here! *(Points in Jamshid's face.)* Did you know that? He could denounce me to the police, I would be arrested for beating my own son, they won't care if he's committed adultery, they all do it! I'll be in prison and he'll be free!

Jamshid: *(Sneering.)* So you're afraid to beat your own son!

Old man: Of course not! He'd never denounce his own father! But that's all I can do. You have no idea, every day I must swallow insults, you must learn to swallow the insults!

Jamshid: Never!

Old man: What else can you do? My daughter, does she wear a veil or even a scarf to cover her hair? No! She refuses and what must I do? Beat her? My son-in-law won't go to the Mosque! What must I do? Drag him there? *(Turns his back on Jamshid and walks towards the window, then he spins round fast, facing Jamshid again.)* Even my grandson has a pet dog!

Jamshid: But something you must do!

Old man: YES! I have three choices, grin and bear it, live alone or return to Iran! *(He steps right up to Jamshid, his eyes boring into his soul.)* Believe me, it's best you keep your mouth shut for the sake of your family, and that is the most you can do.

Jamshid gives up; he believes the old man is a fool, defeated and weak. He knows he won't join him and he has no answer to calm the black pit in his heart. Just swallow down the bitterness and then get on with life.

Jamshid: Shame on you! You are well known for being very religious, but today you give me no help, you are telling me to let them do want they want! I cannot believe it.

Old Man: Do you know what I pray for? No! Of course not, you know nothing about me! You don't know me at all.

Jamshid: At least you know what a no good filthy pig of a son you have!

Old man: I have always known it myself.

Jamshid: You should punish him! Throw him in the street . . . with nothing!

Old man: I should.

Jamshid: But will you?

Old man: *(Staring hard at Jamshid.)* Who can say?

FARUZEH'S BEDROOM /NIGHT
The room is dark; there's a faint streetlight filtering through the curtains and Abbas and Faruzeh are sleeping.

A loud clunking sound of the front door being unlocked wakes the dog and he runs up and down the corridor barking. Abbas wakes up, then a light switch clicks on in the hall and a sharp bright outline appears around the bedroom door. Abbas creeps over to the door and quietly opens it a crack.

CORRIDOR/NIGHT

Old man: THERE YOU ARE! *(A slap and a heavy thud as Hamid falls against the wall.)* YOU SWINE! *(Hamid scrambles backwards along the corridor.)* I had a visitor today…. JAMSHID MOHAMMED! What the hell are you playing at?

Hamid stands cornered in the corridor with a black eye, a shopping bag and his plastic magic charm bracelet on his wrist. He's wearing a tight T-shirt that exposes his stomach with a pair of women's green leggings and rubber flip-flops all borrowed from Patty. Bewildered, he peers at the old man like a son laying eyes on his father for the first time in years. He is dead drunk from Patty's whisky.

Hamid: I've been earning some extra cash teaching English, but I was brought down by a bad woman. *(Shocked by his own confession he falls to his knees.)* Dad, I'm a useless sack of shit! To think I was brought down by a woman who beats up her midget mother-in-law! Sorry Dad.

Old man: SORRY! YOU'RE SORRY? *(He strides towards Hamid and pokes him in the chest with his walking stick.)* Do I care about midgets and mother in laws? Get your arse up!

Hamid doesn't move, if he tries to stand he knows he'll fall. The old man jerks him to his feet by his T-shirt. His shiny, tiny eyes bore into his son's pissed stare for as long at it takes for him to swipe Hamid in the guts with his stick. There's a loud crash and the bikes are falling down in the hall.

Old man: Give me that bag!

Hamid: Leave it Dad; it's just some stuff.

Old man: You think I'm a fool? Yes I am a fool! I went to your dead mother's wardrobe and do you know what I found gone? No STOLEN? *(Spit sprays from his mouth.)* Guess what is missing?

Hamid: Dad it's late. *(The old man lunges for the bag.)* Let it alone….

Abbas steps out the bedroom door, squeezing his eyes against the glare of neon light.

Hamid and the old man are pouring sweat, like two oily djins fighting over a treasure, a magic lamp, an old plastic shopping bag. The old man tears it from Hamid's grasp and pulls out his wife's old black burqa; it smells musty and sad.

Old man: Where did you get it? It's your mother's! ISN'T IT? . . . YOU SWINE!

Hamid: I borrowed it to teach English.

Old man: Teach my arse! *(He cackles.)* Take you out and shoot you that's what I say! Teach my arse!

Faruzeh stands behind Abbas at the bedroom door and Hamid makes a dash for the bathroom. He can climb out the window and escape over the garage roofs like he did as a kid.

Old man: COME BACK HERE!

There is a loud crash and Hamid cries out. Faruzeh follows Abbas into the corridor.

Hamid is standing there holding Hosro's red bike up in front of him as a shield. The old man is hitting at the bike with his walking stick, getting it stuck in the spokes of the wheels. Faruzeh and Abbas watch transfixed as everything moves like an old film reel. The old man keeps bringing his stick down hard, again and again. Hamid holds his bike shield high, warding off the strikes as the old man misses and strikes the hall mirror. An explosion, and the mirror disintegrates. Glittering, splintering shards of glass rain to the floor. He drives Hamid back down the corridor, striking blows on the cross bar, a dull clanging on iron.

Hamid feels himself deflating as his strength leaks out through his pores in bean size drops of sweat, and he watches in dismay as his arms shrivel up like burnt meat. The bike falls and Hamid's heart sizzles like melted rubber in a fire. The stick breaks and the old man is left holding a sharp jagged weapon in his hand. Faced with yet another spike Hamid falls to the floor rolling himself into a hedgehog. He feels a cold hand grab his hair yanking him, making him stand back up, and his body is like a pile of pig's intestines, slipping and sliding back down on the floor, cold slippery innards full of stench and fear with a dagger pointed at his throat. The old man staggers; he stumbles over the bike and grabs Hamid's shoulder, gasping, as he can't get his breath.

Hamid: DAD! . . . DAD?

Hamid tries to support his father but the old man pushes him away and turns instead to the wall. He lets the stick drop. Slowly leaning on the wall to steady himself the old man shuffles stiffly back along the corridor to his room. He holds himself up in the doorframe of his softly lit bedroom. Hosro is awake inside.

Old man: HOSRO! Get my insulin.

Faruzeh: Dad, let him sleep, I'll get it.

The old man goes into his room and shuts the door.

KITCHEN

Faruzeh is preparing the syringe. Abbas is standing at the sink. Hamid comes in carrying a flight holdall and Faruzeh looks at him shaking her head. She passes him a dishtowel.

Faruzeh: You'd better mop yourself up before you leave, or you'll get arrested! You look like you've murdered someone....

Hamid: I'll be back in a few days, when he's calmed down.

Abbas scratches his stomach, gives Hamid a conspiratorial grimace and goes back to his bedroom.

PATTY'S FLAT/NIGHT

The doorbell is ringing; Patty gropes her way along the hall to the front door and fumbles for the light switch. She peeps through the spy hole, sees a dark tubby man all beaten up and then she opens the door.

Hamid: Sorry . . . I need somewhere to stay.

He's looking at her standing in a silk baby doll and pink animal slippers, not sure if they're pigs or hippos.

Patty: Come in.... *(She lets him through, shutting the door behind him.)* You've got beaten up again, did that bloke find you?

Hamid: No it was my dad, this time.

They're sitting at the kitchen table. She opens a bottle of brandy and slides a glass across the table to Hamid, and then she lights a candle.

PARK BENCH/DAY

The old man is sitting with his jacket pulled tightly about him, and Turpin Cyrus Babai sits at his feet on the dusty grass his head on one side, listening.

Old man: I gave him the best name! Our prophet said, 'Give your child a good name.' and what did I do? I gave him the best! A name with number three, so is it my fault? *(He shakes his head.)* No it cannot be! Everybody knows that some of these people with good numbers like one, three and nine, still they are having problems! And why? *(He looks down at the dog.)* I'll tell you, the answer lies in the words of a renowned Islamic scholar. 'Bad marriage combinations can ruin a man for life no matter what his name.'

Turpin Cyrus Babai whines softly.

Old man: *(Patting the dogs head.)* You're right; he's not even married. But I know where he's staying since the fight, with some Kafir woman! He thinks I don't know. *(He slaps his forehead.)* Of course! We must get him away from her. He needs to marry, and we have to find a Muslim girl with the right number. I must not neglect my duties as head of the household. In the end all will come right! Maybe we will find one for Hosro too! Come along....

He stands up and strides towards the blocks of flats on the other side of the park, his back bent and a scruffy dog at his heels.

MARKET CAFE/DUSK
OUTSIDE CAFE

From across the shop there's a fast food cafe with large windows overlooking the street. Hamid is sitting inside next to a window waiting for Amina to arrive. Outside it's dusk. The street lamps are already lit, yet there's still a dull daylight and everything is bathed in an orange glow.

INSIDE CAFE

Hamid has a maxi burger, chips and a milk shake in front of him, there's also a newspaper and a bunch of keys on the table. He watches Amina crossing the road towards the cafe. She comes through the glass swing doors, spots Hamid and sits down opposite him. She has lots of small shopping bags and puts them down on the chair next to her. Nearby, a fat waiter with his face covered in pimples wipes down a table.

Amina: How can you eat this junk? You'll keep on getting fatter! *(She smoothes her skirt over her plump thighs as she crosses her legs.)*

Hamid: *(He looks down and pinches a roll of fat on his stomach.)* Do you want something?

Amina: No, just a tea.

Hamid: *(Calls to the waiter.)* Excuse me. Can we have a pot of tea?

The boy nods and goes over to the counter. Amina takes a chip from Hamid's plate.

Amina: So what have you been getting up to?

Hamid: Nothing much . . . I've moved out. *(He smirks.)*

Amina: What?

Hamid: I'm living with Patty.

Amina: *(Very surprised.)* Why?

Hamid: I can't take living with my old man anymore, the fighting and the arguments. I don't know why I stayed so long, first to keep the peace between him and Faruzeh after she married Abbas. That was hard! Then I got used to being around, sticking up for them and stuff…. You know I actually feel sorry for him.

Amina: Why?

Hamid: We've all let him down somehow, disappointed him, Dad's always been….

Amina: You should've done it years ago, I've told you loads of times. But why did you move in so fast with this Patty girl?

Hamid: Are you jealous?

Amina: Are you in love with her?

Hamid: Yeah.

Amina: Bullshit! No one can fall in love that fast.

Hamid: How do you know what anyone else can do?

Amina: Suit yourself. It's infatuation! Anyway I like her, and I'm not jealous, never have been and never will be! *(She narrows her eyes at Hamid.)* Huh really! *(She tilts* *her head back.)* Actually I've decided to become a nun, I'm sick of men.

Hamid: No one as greedy as you can stay sick for long.

Amina: Huh!

They smile because they know what the other's thinking. Amina kicks his legs under the table, eats the chips off his plate and winks at the fat spotty boy when he brings the tea. The boy gets red and leaves the tray on the table. Hamid looks at his watch.

Hamid: I'm taking Patty to Reza's for dinner. *(He slides the bunch of keys across the table to her.)* Here are the keys, I'll make up for it, I'll do Thursdays lesson on my own OK? *(He spoons heaps of sugar into her cup and pours the tea.)*

Amina: No need to, I'm going to Iran for a few weeks in May, so then you can hold the fort for me. *(She takes another chip from his plate.)* Carla said she'll give you a hand and I hope you'll keep all our girls happy.

Hamid: *(He drops his head in his hands.)* Agh! Thanks a lot! *(He sits back up and sucks his milk shake through the straw making a gurgling sound.)* Are you going to visit your parents?

Amina: Yes and my sisters and nieces and everyone else too. *(She lights a cigarette exhaling a cloud of smoke between her and Hamid.)* Oh! Guess who's shut up shop suddenly? *(Hamid shrugs.)* Jamshid Mohammed . . . the creep, you remember? *(Hamid's face is blank.)* Come on.... The one with the carpet shop in Black Street, he's left the boys with his father, put his mother in an old peoples home and rushed off to Iran with his wife. No one knows why, nor for how long, probably for a death.

Hamid's face feels like stone, blood pounding in his ears.

Amina: Hey, what's wrong?

Hamid: Nothing. *(He looks down at his plate, at the burger bitten and torn, splattered with red ketchup.)*

Amina: Look, I've got to go. *(She takes the keys and tosses them in her bag.)* I've still got to buy shoes for all my nieces; I've a list a mile long. I sometimes wonder why you never go back to Tehran? You can get really cheap tickets!

Hamid: I was too young when we left, I don't remember anyone. My uncle still goes back for family gatherings, even Faruzeh and Abbas went for a wedding last year, but not me! I made myself a promise I'd never go back.

Hamid remembers the leaving. First his father had disappeared and no one would say why. 'Baba's gone away.' 'When will he come back?' 'Cant say, be a good boy.' Alone at night Maman cried, it wasn't the first time, the aunts said she was as parched and plain as the desert and needed the wetness. Uncles whispered on the roof at night, then Behdad Babai returned to his family home. Hamid saw his father's homecoming from the window on a dark black night. He heard the screech of rubber tires and an old black van skidded to a halt in the road. The back doors opened and something all broken was rolled out, a lump chucked in the road and the van was gone. The lump lie there and then his uncles came and carried the twisted thing into house and Baba was home again. But now they were told to stay inside and not to step out on the sunlit streets anymore. Baba looked ugly, all purple and black, he got fired and was no longer the schoolmaster.

All this Hamid knew from listening to the whispers that blew like a breeze through the house and by leaning over the walls and peering through the bars of the gate. He came to know that Bolour the pretty girl down the road has lost her face, it was burnt away with acid and Maman and the aunts became afraid. Now they were leaving for England. Suitcases were packed, they had to leave it all behind, no room for all those small scraps of life. Do not look back and Behdad Babai sold the house to a cousin for a song, no time to lose and no money. One day in the late afternoon they left for the airport. Behdad borrowed an old van not unlike the one he'd been delivered home in a few months before. Hamid and his sister were squashed in the back, their legs glued to the hot seat. Their mother sat between them and their father stood on the dusty street. He was shaking hands, kissing and saying his farewells to them all. As his father stood in the crowd crushed between neighbours and family, people stared at him in reverence and fear. Men touched him, women watched him, and his mother gazed down at her twisted hands as they lay motionless in her lap. His mother's thin lips tightened when a girl in a virginal white dress with long golden tresses flowing over her shoulders pushed her way through the crowd. Her eyes behind her black veil pouring tears like raindrops soaking her breasts. She elbowed her way through the people and called like a lark. 'Behdad, Behdad.' It was the sweetest voice and the crowd turned; they waited for Behdad to acknowledge her presence, even if only from the corner of his eyes.

A girl he had fed with fresh mulberries at dawn, mulberries still cool from the night air, shaken from an old tree heavy with deep red mulberries. She and he had stood together watching them fall. They could just taste each mulberry as they fell on the snow-white shawl he had lain at the foot of the gnarled tree trunk. They had devoured cool sweet juicy mulberries under an orange sky as the sun rose, their mouths smeared red as they lay by a silver stream on a white shawl stained red, and the wind had stirred the leaves as they rustled and gently fluttered in the breeze. But Behdad did not turn to look at her, his face grew as red as the sunrise they had lain under, and he kept his eyes straight ahead. He turned his newly bent back that would never straighten and climbed into the van, he gripped the steering wheel and hit the gas. Bolour called him again, her hand nearly touching the dirt cold steel of the van as Behdad Babai drove away into the red sunset, onward and onward, and he and his van became one with the red wheel of the sun. Then London where he became a shopkeeper and his wife died of shame. Only he remembers the smell of Tehran, and the sky was blue, it was always blue.

ROAD OUTSIDE CAFE/NIGHT
Now it's dark outside. Hamid comes through the glass doors onto the street; he's not looking where he's going, not taking anything in. He steps into the road. A car swerves in front of him, tyres screeching. The car skids towards him, Hamid freezes, throwing his arms up in front of his face, he screws his eyes shut waiting for the hit.
The car bumps to a halt on the opposite kerb. The driver furiously winds down the window. Hamid opens his eyes, letting his arms drop.
Driver: YOU STUPID BASTARD! LOOK WHERE YOU'RE GOING! *(He restarts the car.)* FUCKING ASSHOLE!
The car drives off and Hamid, shaken, crosses the road to his scooter.

OUTSIDE SHOP/DAY
The old man is walking down the street wearing a long tunic, a jacket and a fez hat.
He goes up to the shop door and looks at the dance class poster; the other for private lessons is no longer there. He pushes the door open and steps inside.
Hamid is behind the counter he looks up seeing his father come in.
Hamid: Dad! What are you doing here, is there a problem? Are you well?

98

Old man: NO! I'm sick and old . . . and alone. Can't an old man come and find his own son?

Hamid: Of course Dad.

Old man: I never see you anymore.

Hamid: *(Resigned he shakes his head.)* Dad, that's not true. I come home every day after I shut the shop.

Old man: *(Voice querulous and whining.)* It's not the same. You stay out all night now. Don't even get back for morning prayers…. *(Hamid fusses around in the counter drawer, not wanting to meet his father's gaze.)* Do you know? I'd wake most nights, I still do, can't sleep. I used to watch you sleeping . . . it made me feel comfy.

Hamid: *(Uncomfortable.)* You don't need to watch me sleeping Dad, you can watch Hosro now.

Old man: Agh! He's changed. *(The old man jabs his finger in the air.)* Become sneaking he has, just like a serpent…. Now I sit in bed at night, and instead of watching my son I have to see my grandson masturbating away, because he thinks I'm sleeping. Is that a life for me?

Hamid: *(Moving away he goes to tidy the newspaper stand.)* Dad! Look, sell the flat! Faruzeh can sell the house in Wimbledon, even with a sitting tenant it has to be worth something. You could get a bigger flat together, have your own bedroom.

Old man: Rubbish, they'll have to carry me out in a coffin, and when I'm dead and buried you can do what you want with my flat. *(Following Hamid.)* Hmm, listen Hamid…. Drop these ridiculous dance classes, they make us look foolish.

Hamid: No Dad. Is this why you came?

Old man: Perhaps? Actually I came here because I want you to be at home for Sunday lunch. I want to have a family meal all together.

Hamid: Can I bring Patty?

Old man: No you bloody well can't, Patty my arse!
I don't know her and I don't want her. It's a family lunch.

BABAI FLAT/DAY
SITTING ROOM
The dining table is set for nine; there's a banquet laid out with dishes filled with saffron rice, chicken baked with walnuts and pomegranate, bowls filled with yoghurt, mint and cucumbers, fragrant herb omelettes, aubergine dips, and cups of creamy rice puddings with rose water.
There are extra chairs in front of the television forming a circle and Turpin Cyrus Babai is asleep on his own settee, which has been wedged in between the table and the old man's chair. The television is on, showing a re-run of Dallas. Hamid is sitting on one of the chairs smoking, then Faruzeh walks in bringing a large platter of koofteh berenji rice balls to the table.

Hamid: Who are the others?

Faruzeh: I don't know, some distant relatives? It's supposed to be a surprise.

Hamid shakes his head slowly and draws deeply on his cigarette.

OLD MAN'S BEDROOM
The old man is knotting Hosro's tie while Hosro stands resigned and sulking. His hair is spiky with Brylcreem.

Old man: That's no way to have a hairstyle! *(Shakes his head.)* Tsk, a freaks style. Looks as if you've been electrocuted!

Hosro: *(Moodily under his breath.)* And you'd know just how they look.

The old man ignores him and takes a big comb from his dresser and flattens down Hosro's hair with a side parting, he then hands him a magnified shaving mirror.

Hosro peers at himself, his nose elongated and hair greased down.

Hosro: *(Panic.)* I'm not coming out like this! I look a real creep!

Old man: Hah! You looked a bloody creep before! Now, shape up! Millions of people all around the world have ridiculous hairstyles, look at your father! But those who become bloody pop stars are rare, it's a matter of fate. It's all in your bones, if you're born with the bones of a beggar, that's how you'll spend your life!

The doorbell rings, the old man spits on his hanky and hurriedly polishes the gold buttons on his embroidered jacket. He swipes at his beard with a hair brush like he's swatting at flies, then hurries out the door leaving Hosro standing there alone.

SITTING ROOM

An old couple are sitting on the sofa; the woman, Mummy Akbar, is as fat as a pig and pyramid shaped, with a pea brain head and arse as wide as a sea cow. She's wearing a headscarf tied under her chins, tight enough to hold them up and keep them off her chest.

Her husband, Mr Akbar, is a skinny old man with shiny old medals pinned to his chest.

Sitting on the kitchen chairs facing them are the daughter and niece. They're wearing identical red trouser suits, sporting the same beehive hairdo's with three ringlets hanging down each side framing their faces, they look like plaster window dummies. Fatima, sixteen years old, and fat just like her mummy, has thick make up on her face, lipstick on her mouth and she's showing off her red lips and white teeth. The niece Hafsa is over thirty, her neck is long and thin like a plucked chicken with mottled green and purple skin marked by seven black moles. She has a beaky nose, her lips hang slack and her bulbous eyes just stare straight ahead like a blind bat.

Behind Hafsa, the television is still on and everyone has to shout a bit to be heard. Hamid and Faruzeh are folding napkins at the table. The old man is standing in front of the Akbars showing them photographs when Hosro enters with his hair spiked up.

Old man: Ahh, my grandson! *(He takes hold of Hosro's shoulder pushing him in front of the Akbars.)* Hosro's nearly seventeen, a fine young man, eh? *(He gestures towards the Akbars.)* You remember Mr Hussein Akbar? Meet his good lady, their daughter Fatima and their niece Hafsa! *(He doesn't bother to turn towards Hafsa, in fact he's standing in front of her, blocking her from view.)*

Mr Akbar: *(Stands up and shakes Hosro's hand.)* Heeloo! *(In a singsong voice.)* My how you've grown, what? We haven't seen you since Babeck's wedding…. Five years ago, how time flies. *(He continues pumping Hosro's hand shaking him to pieces.)*

Mummy Akbar: *(From her chair.)* Hello.

Fatima: Hello.

The old man shoves Hosro down on the chair next to Fatima.

Hafsa: *(From behind the old man.)* Hello.

The old man drops the pile of photos in Hosro's lap.

Old man: Take a look at your cousin's wedding photographs. *(Looking at the Akbars.)* Practically the same age you know, Hosro and his cousin. *(Looking down at Hosro.)* Shame your parents didn't take you.

Faruzeh: *(From across the room.)* It was in Tehran during the school term.

Old man: Abdul went! *(Turning to the Akbars.)* Hosro is studying for his A levels, then off to study medicine or engineering. Huh? What do you have to say Hosro?

Hosro is sitting staring ahead, his face red and shining; he has the photos clutched in his hands.

KITCHEN

Abbas is at the stove; he's wearing tight jeans and an apron over his Japanese kimono jacket. His face is greasy and he looks stressed. On the kitchen table are two baking trays of pistachio and almond baklava.

Faruzeh: *(From the corridor.)* ABBAS?

Faruzeh and then Hamid arrive in the kitchen.

Faruzeh: Have you seen what's happening? That Fatima girl and her bloody parents!

Abbas: So what?

Faruzeh: So what? *(She huffs impatiently.)* Don't you see what he's up to? *(She begins to cut up the baklava into squares.)* He's interfering, trying to marry Hosro.

Abbas: Huh, it's just a coincidence. *(Abbas keeps frying his rice balls not taking his eyes from the pan.)*

Faruzeh: You heard him Hamid! *(She mimics the old man's voice.)* 'Cousin's wedding, they're the same age.' Hosro's going to be a bloody doctor now! Or was it engineer?

Hamid is looking in the fridge; he finds a can of Coke and drinks.

SITTING ROOM

Hosro sits rigidly on his chair passing round the family photos, while the Akbars coo and cackle at every picture. Hafsa is carefully picking her ear. Fatima twiddles one of her ringlets around her finger, sneaking looks at Hosro.

Old man: Tsk tsk! Well there's a thing…. You just never can tell.

Akbars: *(Laugh in unison.)*

Hosro sees Fatima looking at him, she makes a sulky moue and Hosro looks away. The old man gets up.

Old man: One moment please. *(He leaves the room.)*

Mr Akbar: Well Hosro, and what have you to say about yourself…. We're waiting…. What? *(He cups his hand around his ear.)*

Mummy Akbar and the two girls laugh like braying donkeys.

KITCHEN

Now all four are in the kitchen. Faruzeh is standing with her hands on her hips.

Old man: And what's wrong? So what if I have? That girl is a nice good girl and her parents are related. It's time he was introduced to some decent families. He must meet the right kind of girl, I have checked her numbers and astrology says yes!

Faruzeh: Are you mad? He's only sixteen. We are not living a hundred years ago.

Old man: Nonsense! There is no harm. I am the head of the family I will decide!

Hamid: Dad's right, I think she looks lovely. She'll make a fine bride for Hosro.

Abbas and Hamid double over laughing. The old man is furious.

Old man: *(He jabs his finger at Hamid.)* You! After the trouble you've made, better for you to get to know the niece, I have chosen her for you!

Hamid: Please Dad, not Chicken woman!

Abbas hoots with laughter, Faruzeh giggles. The old man bangs his fist down on the table.

Old man: *(To Abbas.)* YOU SHUT YOUR FACE! HOW DARE YOU…. *(He clutches the front of Abbas's apron, half hanging on.)* You married MY daughter, without MY permission. Do you think I'd have chosen an Ass like you?

Abbas steps backwards trying to pull his apron from the old man's grasp.

Old man: Cretin! Moron! Nerd! Ninny! Simpleton! Clod! Dumbass! Dunce…. *(Abbas jerks his apron from the old man's grip, pushing him backwards.)* Right! You want to have another fight? *(Snatches the knife off the table, jeering.)* I haven't forgotten the cassette player fat boy! You're a long haired twit, you need a haircut. *(He starts waving the knife at Abbas who backs up towards the door.)* Ha ha! Like a schoolgirl with a stupid ponytail…. It needs chopping off!

He charges at Abbas who ducks sideways just as Mummy Akbar walks into the kitchen. The old man stumbles forwards with the knife in his hand. He collides with Mummy Akbar, she screams, falling backwards on the kitchen floor and the old man lands on top of her. Then he scrambles to his feet, winded, and chucks the knife in the sink.

Old man: *(Facing Abbas.)* This is all your fault! *(He points to Mummy Akbar on the floor.)* Lucky for you she doesn't have a scratch on her!

CORRIDOR

The sitting room door opens, out comes Mr Akbar with the girls and Hosro. They crowd in the kitchen doorway staring at Mummy Akbar lying on the floor.

Old man: Carry her to the couch! Carry her through! Just fainted, that's all.

Hafsa: What happened?

Old man: Maybe she's fainted from hunger, she just fell down when she walked in. Hamid you take her by the left! *(The old man lifts under her right arm.)* HOSRO LEGS!

They struggle to lift her off the floor; she's slippery like cow tripe. They finally get a hold of her. Hosro has lifted her legs up, and to get the leverage he's standing squashed between them. Her skirt falls back and she's wearing stockings and suspenders over her bulging flesh, Hafsa darts forward, hurriedly pulling Mummy Akbar's skirt back up.

Mr Akbar: *(Standing in the corridor with his arms folded.)* Get a grip! HOLD TIGHT…. Mind her now.

The old man and Hamid have her under the armpits. They sway and strain carrying her down the corridor, her bottom dragging along the floor as they go. At the doorway they bash her head really hard on the frame.

Mr Akbar: Be careful!

Fatima: Ooh her head! *(She clings on to Hafsa.)*

SITTING ROOM

They struggle across the room to the sofa. The old man gives out and lets go, she slips out of Hamid's grasp and with her legs still wrapped around Hosro's thighs her head drops on the floor.

Mr Akbar: Careful now, nice and easy does it.

Fatima: Agh! Mummy?

The old man is bent over winded and Hamid has staggered back and sat in a chair. The Three Akbars are standing together in the doorway; Hafsa has her arm around Fatima. Hosro is stooped over Mummy Akbar still holding her legs, and then he drops them on the sofa as if they were old dead fish.

Old man: *(Straightening up, panting out of breath.)* That's right Hosro! Legs up, head down, perfect position to recover from a fainting fit. A cushion for her head! *(He looks at the Akbars.)* Not to worry … to overcome a faint … the legs must be kept above the head.

Mummy Akbar is lying twisted on the floor with her legs up on the sofa. The old man takes a cushion and pulls her head up by the hair and shoves the cushion underneath.

Fatima: MUMMY?

Hafsa: *(Still hugging Fatima to her.)* Uncle, don't you think we should call an ambulance?

Mr Akbar: *(Bewildered.)* Umm.…

Old man: Nonsense! She'll come round soon enough.… Not a scratch on her, as I said, she fell on the floor as she walked in the kitchen. Well Hussein, shall we eat? Lots of delicious food sitting there waiting for us, what?

They slowly take their places and sit down to eat; Abbas and Faruzeh have stayed in the kitchen, Hosro creeps towards the door.

Old man: HOSRO, come and eat!

Hosro sits down. Everyone eats in silence except the old man, who chews with his mouth open and makes loud sucking sounds throughout the meal.

Mr Akbar: Not coming to eat your son-in-law?

Old man: Can't he's got a weak stomach!

Mummy Akbar reaches her arm in the air as though waving, unnoticed by anyone. She makes kicking movements, pawing with her feet like she's pedaling a bicycle and then she lies still.

Mr Akbar: And your daughter?

Old man: Tsk! She must attend to him. *(He nods his head slowly as though meditating the fact.)*

Fatima is looking at Hosro. She's winding her ringlet round and round her finger and giving him coy looks from across the table.

Turpin Cyrus Babai is seated under the table next to the old man's legs, devouring the tiny fried meatballs the old man tosses under the tablecloth for him.

Old man: *(He notices Hafsa looking at him sourly.)* No need to disapprove, not at all! This dog is not a pet but a guard dog. Recently there have been a lot of houses broken into, even in the middle of the night.

Mr Akbar: Dogs should be kept outside, even guard dogs.

Old man: How? We live in a flat!

Hafsa: He seems too small for a guard dog, don't you think Uncle?

Mr Akbar ignores her and keeps on eating.

Old man: Maybe he is small, but never judge by the size! He also barks every time someone passes by in the hall, now that's useful as a warning isn't it?

Hafsa: I should think it must be very annoying, I expect in a block of flats like this he must be barking on and off all day.

Old man: Well maybe he is, and maybe he isn't.

Mr Akbar: Hafsa, please do not argue this issue! *(He turns to the old man.)* Women need husbands or they start to bicker and think they are equal to a man! Ahh! This is delicious, I must compliment your daughter's cooking!

Old man: A family recipe, my wife, hers were . . . tsk . . . more clover! Faruzeh now . . . hmm, just so-so. Now tell me about your plans, I too have been considering opening a new business, maybe some laundry service or this pizza delivery franchise....

Hosro is staring at his plate ignoring Fatima who's now winding ringlets round her fingers on both sides of her head.

Fatima: I want to go home!

Mr Akbar: What! What's this?

Fatima: I want to go home and NOW!

Mr Akbar: Nonsense! Shut up. *(He turns back to his plate and carries on eating.)*

Fatima: *(Fatima looks angrily at Hosro.)* He made a rude face at me and he did this. *(She holds up her hands, curling her left hand into a tunnel, she feverishly pumps her right index finger in and out the hole mimicking sexual intercourse.)*

The old man jumps up and lands a heavy clout round Hosro's head. Hamid stands up.

Hamid: Dad, leave him alone…. I don't believe he did that!

Hosro: *(Wiping his eyes.)* I didn't.

Mr Akbar: *(Stands up.)* Are you calling my daughter a liar?

Hamid: She's just mistaken that's all.

Hafsa: Don't forget Uncle, Fatima and the Kebab boy, she made that up!

Mr Akbar: Shut your mouth! *(Ignoring Hamid, he leans into Hosro's face.)* Did you or did you not make that disgusting sign to my daughter? *(When he says 'disgusting' some spit lands on Hosro's face.)*

Hosro: *(He jumps up.)* I feel sick! *(He wipes his face and stumbles out the room.)*

The table is silent. Hamid, Mr Akbar and the old man are still standing. Fatima sits sulking with her arms crossed and Hafsa chews down the Baklava faster than a rabbit.

Mr Akbar: Well I never…. *(He kicks back his chair, it falls.)* Fatima, Hafsa thank Mr Babai for such a wonderful lunch…. We're leaving!

Hafsa: What about Auntie?

They all turn to look at Mummy Akbar forgotten on the floor, she hasn't moved. Mr Akbar takes a jug of water from the table and goes over to her.

Mr Akbar: Maimuna? *(He stares down at her, prodding her with his foot.)* MAIMUNA ENOUGH!

Still she doesn't move but her eyelids flicker. Mr Akbar pours water down on her face from his standing position. It splashes heavily streaking her face with blotches of make up that run down her cheeks. She now looks like a gargoyle.

Hafsa: Uncle, I think you'd better call an ambulance!

Mr Akbar: Very well, if I must! *(Unconvinced, he turns to Hamid.)* Where's the telephone?

Hamid: In the hall.

CORRIDOR

Mr Akbar comes into the corridor. Faruzeh is leaning against the wall talking and laughing on the phone. Mr Akbar coughs loudly and she turns round looking sharply at him.

Faruzeh: What do you want?

Mr Akbar: An Ambulance.

Hafsa: *(Calls from sitting room.)* Uncle! Auntie's come round.

STAIRWAY DOWN TO GROUND FLOOR

Hamid and Abbas are supporting Mummy Akbar as she limps between them. Her husband is following behind with the girls. Mummy Akbar makes little squeals like a stuck pig.

Mr Akbar: Steady! Steady! That's right! Steady now.

The girls hang onto each other exclaiming 'Ooh and Ahh' as Mummy Akbar is bumped down the stairs.

FRONT DOOR

The Akbars are driving off in their saloon. Hamid and Abbas are coming back up the steps.

PATTY'S FLAT SITTING ROOM/NIGHT

Hamid is making up someone to be. He sits on the edge of a chair twiddling invisible glossy black ringlets, he simpers and blushes then jumps up and cuffs himself round the ear. Now he's a blubber woman and waddles across the sitting room, he slashes about with an invisible knife and reels over backwards. Then he drags his fat carcass to the sofa and sticks his legs up in the air waving them in silly circles riding a bicycle. He jumps up and kicks the blubber woman on the floor and chucks water on her from his unseeable jug, while patty giggles and claps her hands, delighted by his performance.

BABAI FLAT/DAY
BASEMENT

Hamid is moving boxes looking for a suitcase; eventually he finds a battered Pullman with missing wheels. Inside are some kids clothes, letters tied together with string and old family photograph albums. Hamid opens a trunk next to him full of newspapers, and he stuffs the clothes and bundles of letters in on top and shuts the trunk. He sits down on the lid to look through the faded photos of family weddings and birthdays in Tehran in the 1970s. Everyone is smiling, all dressed in their best fancy clothes with shining faces. There's a photo of Faruzeh in her school uniform with her hair braided, and he remembers another picture he has of her in his memory. Every day after school, Faruzeh using a broom as a microphone, singing in front of the mirror with her skirt hitched up. He flips through the pages looking at more photos. There's one of his father standing with his brothers. They're all wearing white papakhi hats, the long tendrils of curly lambs wool framing their heads like wild Afros. In another Hamid sees himself, standing under a Date tree with a bow and arrow aiming at the distant Alborz Mountain. He puts the albums in the flap of the suitcase and shuts it up. He takes one last look around.

OLD MAN'S BEDROOM

The old man is sitting in bed reading a newspaper and eating sweets from a tin. His hand goes from tin to mouth to tin, tossing sweets in his gob and chewing as fast as Turpin Cyrus Babai who's sitting on Hamid's bed. Hamid is emptying a chest of drawers, putting piles of ironed clothes into his suitcase while the old man takes no notice of him.

Hamid closes the case and straightens up.

Hamid: Dad? I'm off now, I'll drop in after work on Monday . . . Dad, I'm off!

Old man: You're not OFF! Do not speak to me as though you are just going out and will be home later! I know you are living with that Kafir woman! You have left your home and never had the guts to say so!

Hamid: Dad, that's not fair. *(He looks guilty.)* Look would you like me to sleep here tonight?

Old man: Don't bother, I don't need your pity!

Hamid: Anyway you gave my bed to Turpin weeks ago and don't deny it Dad. Look at him! He's become as fat as a baby pig.

Old man: Don't talk rubbish I have not given him your bed! How many times do I have to tell you all, he's just a guard dog! I need him in the room at night. I have been informed that dogs are famous for alerting their owners to gas leaks, fires, heart attacks and the like, and at my age I need him as extra security.

Hamid: You didn't have to give him my bed. He could sleep on the floor!

Old man: I haven't given him your bed, nonsense!

Hamid: Then why has my bed got a fluffy blanket printed with dog paw patterns? And why is there a black and white Dalmatian bedside lamp with a Cruella de Vil lampshade? Anyway you should get rid of it, Cruella used dogs to make fur coats, and it might give poor little Turpin nightmares!

Old man: Hosro chose the blanket! Nothing to do with me, and who is this Cruella?

Hamid: She's a villain in a dog film, ask Hosro….

Old man: Just get on with your packing, leave if you must but you're not taking Cyrus with you.

Hamid: I don't want him.

Old man: He's the only one who listens to me, just think of that! I have a family, but the only one I can talk to is a dog and he's not even permitted! *(The old man goes back to reading his newspaper.)*

Hamid: I'll be in after work . . . every day, same as usual I promise. *(Softly.)* Look Dad, why don't you get a hobby?

Old man: Hobby my arse! . . . Hobbies are for idiots who have nothing better to do! Out of here and take your suitcase with you!

The old man turns his back on Hamid, rolling over upsetting the sweets on the bed. Hamid picks them up and puts them back on the bedside table. He leaves the room, returning a moment later with a gigantic canary yellow ghetto blaster with a red ribbon tied in a bow on the handle.

Hamid: Dad, look I've bought you a present....

Old man: *(His back to Hamid.)* Don't want a bloody present. I'm not a child, I'm not bloody gaga yet!

Hamid: You don't know what it is! *(He presses play and muezzin chanting starts. The old man turns round sitting up. Hamid stops the cassette.)* I bought you a brand new tape too!

Old man: It's enormous, and it's bright yellow, bloody ridiculous!

Hamid: I can take it back and get you a smaller one....

Old man: I don't want you wasting time running backwards and forwards to the shops. I suppose I'll get used to it. How many decibels?

Hamid: A lot, it's the loudest they had in the store!

Old man: Put it under my bed, before that buffoon Abbas gets sight of it! *(He lies back down.)* I'm running low on sweets, Faruzeh has put me on rations. Bring me some extra tins of Okho Chi next time!

Hamid: OK, I'll see you on Monday.... *(He pats the old man and then pats the dog, picks up his suitcase and leaves quietly closing the door behind him.)*

When the door shuts the old man sits back up. He looks at the dog sitting on Hamid's bed.

Old man: Cyrus, you see what an ungrateful son I have? You were abandoned by your master and I by my son! We both know what it is to nurse a viper in our bosom!

PATTY'S FLAT SITTING ROOM/NIGHT
Hamid comes into the room followed by Patty. He's giggling.
Hamid: Well? Where is it?
Patty steps up on to the sofa wobbling on the cushions. There is a canvass hanging on the wall above the sofa covered by a flowery bed sheet.
Hamid: *(Delighted.)* My portrait?
Patty pulls the bed sheet away to reveal Hamid's portrait. The back ground is a streaky brown and yellow. A fat brown man 'Hamid' with bushy black hair and a gold crown, wearing a stripy shirt and flared trousers is standing in profile with a huge erect penis in bright pink poking out of his flies.
There's a queue of twenty matchstick women with sketchily drawn breasts and hair waiting in a long line that crosses the canvass. They're carrying gifts, a roasted turkey on a platter, a velvet box with a gold necklace, a large bottle of whisky and wads of cash. The portrait has been painted scruffily and out of perspective and Hamid is struck.
Hamid: It's beautiful…. It's my life!
He looks at Patty feeling passion. Patty falls backwards on the sofa and Hamid closes in.

BABAI FLAT/DAY
OLD MAN'S BEDROOM
The old man's alarm clock rings; he gets up and pulls the cassette player out from under his bed, he puts his false teeth in and peers at Hosro who's still sleeping. Then

114

carrying his new canary yellow cassette player, he proudly walks bare foot into the sitting room.

SITTING ROOM

He puts the cassette player on top of the television, presses play and turns the volume up full blast. He steps onto his prayer mat then he slaps his forehead, turning round he goes over to the dining table where there's a jug of water. He dips his hand inside and splashes water over his face and then sits down on the chair and splashes water on his feet, after he dips both hands in the jug. Shaking his hands he walks back over to the carpet. He begins bowing and praying when the ceiling cracks like a bolt of lightening and the cathedral chandelier crashes down on top of him in a rain of plaster and splintering glass. He lies there underneath the mound of rubble, twisted metal and smashed light bulbs; a dust cloud billows around the room like thick smoke. He struggles to wake himself but old nightmares and dead memories pull him back.

There's a mullah on a platform shrieking and there's a crowd of filthy men shoving each other scrambling to see the show. The prisoner is brought below the platform while the mullah rants through his distorted megaphone, his voice harsh and rusting, and the crowd are roaring. Behdad is stood against the concrete wall below the platform, his arms held by the men above him. He looks upwards, one fleeting glance at the face of his judge, he sees his eyes shot with blood, his black tongue thrashing and spitting. His gaze drops as his cheek grazes the rough wall splattered with dried blood the colour of brown shit and the stench of urine and fear floods his senses. Down on the dry dirt ground a man starts to flog him, the whip is long and blood blossoms across his back flowering like red corn poppies, the flowers of love, as he writhes and twists his back turns as red as the juice of a mulberry.

Hosro, then Abbas and Faruzeh run in through the door still in their pyjamas. Hosro kneels down by the old man while Abbas struggles to pull the chandelier off him.

Hosro: Call the Doctor! He's unconscious!

Faruzeh turns off the cassette player then she hurries into the hallway.

Abbas: Shall we carry him to the bedroom?

Abbas carefully picks lumps of rubble from him and then they turn him over. Abbas lifts him under his armpits and Hosro takes him by his legs and straining and swaying they carry him out through the doorway.

OLD MAN'S BEDROOM

Faruzeh: *(Entering the bedroom.)* The Doctor's coming right now before he starts his rounds….

They stand around the old man's bed watching him.

Abbas: Look, Hosro and I will get dressed before he gets here….

Faruzeh: Can you call Hamid . . . and Uncle Aziz!

Hosro pulls some clothes from his wardrobe drawer and follows Abbas out the door leaving Faruzeh alone with the old man. She rummages in the bedside table drawer and takes out a tortoiseshell hairbrush and gently brushes her father's matted hair.

SITTING ROOM

Abbas pulls the enormous chandelier into the corner; he has a dustpan and a broom and starts sweeping up the slithers of broken glass and powdered rubble.

Hamid: *(Bursting through the door.)* What the hell happened?

Abbas: *(Stops sweeping.)* The chandelier fell down on him this morning while he was praying.

Hamid: *(Shaking head.)* Why the hell did he buy it? I told him it was too heavy for the ceiling, it's a bloody cathedral chandelier!

Abbas: He loved it, it had a thousand watts!

Hamid: What did the Doctor say?

Abbas: *(Shrugs.)* Just concussion, but he's slipping fast. The doctor said from kidney failure, liver failure, weak heart and old age, he said it would be kinder to let him die at home. His insulin levels are through the roof!

OLD MAN'S BEDROOM

Hamid walks into the bedroom. Hosro and Faruzeh are sitting on the dog's zed bed. Hamid squeezes in and sits down between them wrapping his arms around them, hugging them tight.

Hamid: *(To Faruzeh.)* How is he?

Faruzeh: He's coming and going, we've called Uncle Aziz, he's on his way here.

Hamid: Why don't you and Hosro take a break, I'll stay with him. *(Faruzeh ignores him.)* Go on, you're still in your nightdress....

Faruzeh: *(She gets up and strokes Hosro's head.)* Come and help me prepare some food. *(Faruzeh and Hosro leave the bedroom and Hamid moves over to sit on his father's bed.)*

Hamid: *(Gently shaking the old man's shoulder.)* Dad, can you hear me? *(The old man's eyes open and he lifts his head up off the pillow.)* Dad, you're awake! Say something, Dad?

Old man: Help me sit up. *(Hamid pulls him forwards and plumps up the pillows behind his head, then lets him back down.)* Ouch! Be more careful.

Hamid: Dad, you've come round, you're going to be all right!

Old man: All right my arse! I heard the doctor, I'm done for, I'm like an old banger, not worth repairing,

117

nothing to be done! *(Doorbell rings.)* Don't let that fool Aziz come in here! I don't want him.

Hamid: Dad? How can you say that when he's your own brother?

Old man: Don't care!

Abbas brings uncle Aziz into the bedroom. He's a tall thin man wearing a dark tunic and a fez hat. He's clutching a leather bound Quran to his chest.

Abbas: Thank you for coming. *(He pulls over a chair next to the bed.)* Please sit, we thought you'd be hungry so Faruzeh is preparing some food. I'll call you when it's ready.

Uncle Aziz: Well brother I have come. *(He sits down on the chair and turns to Hamid.)* Sit on the other bed. It's not right to sit upon the bed of a dying man!

Old man: I want him on the bed and I want Cyrus too.

Uncle Aziz: Who is this Cyrus?

Old man: Never you mind, keep your nose out my business, I'm perfectly well, just a false alarm. I'm not dying so you can go and stuff your face along with my donkey son-in-law, and then go back to where you came from.

Uncle Aziz: Bitter as ever! Not even in the jaws of death can you hold your tongue, you even begrudge me a little rice!

Old man: Bitter! And why not? Here I am dying, has anyone asked me if I'm hungry? No they haven't! Even a condemned murderer gets his last supper, anything he wants, and they even have caviar and champagne on death row in America!

Uncle Aziz: You'll not swerve me from my duty, I have come here to recite the Surah thirty-six and I shall whisper the Shahadah as is prescribed. *(He opens the Quran and starts flicking through the pages.)*

Old man: *(To Hamid.)* Go and fetch Cyrus, it's my only hope…. *(Hamid goes out into the sitting room, picks the dog* *up off the settee and carries him into the bedroom and puts him on the bed.)*

Uncle Aziz: What is this abomination? How dare you! *(Looking at Hamid.)* Take this filthy dog from my sight or I will leave this cursed home right now!

Old man: Hamid sit down on the bed too! Your uncle Aziz is going!

Uncle Aziz slams the Quran shut and stands up shaking his head in disbelief. Abbas can hear them quarrelling; he hurries along the corridor and stands just outside the bedroom door peering in.

Uncle Aziz: *(Jabbing his finger at Hamid.)* You have failed your father! You fail in your duties as a son! You are pandering to the whims of a senile confused old man. *(Points to the old man.)* And you are condemning yourself to the lowest pit of hell! Hypocrisy is the most dangerous sin. You claim to believe! Yet you denounce your faith and all that is good with this filthy dog's presence. You'll go to Hawiyah!

Old man: Get out!

Uncle Aziz turns and leaves nearly colliding with Abbas in the doorway. Abbas enters the old man's bedroom quietly.

Hamid: Dad what's going on?

Old man: A thousand watt chandelier fell on my head, what do you expect? I don't want bloody prayers. I want a drink! Ahh! I remember the taste, whisky, I used to drink whisky, and you didn't know that did you? It's the one thing I want now!

Abbas: Maybe he's delirious....

Hamid: Maybe he isn't! Look go and fetch that bottle we keep under the kitchen sink. *(Abbas shrugs, shaking his head, he lumbers out the door.)* I never knew you drank Dad. *(Looking at the old man in wonderment.)*

Old man: I didn't want you to know I was a bad man! All these years I have believed it, but you know what? *(He* *clutches Hamid by his shirt, clinging on.)* Maybe I'm not bad? Maybe we're not bad! *(He falls back on the pillows, letting go of Hamid.)* You've never been a bad son, just a fool. We're all fools! And do you know Hamid? I think it's a good thing to be! *(He grabs hold of Hamid's shirt pulling himself up.)* Can you believe I committed adultery? *(Hamid shakes his head.)* Well I did, for seven weeks! I met a beautiful girl under a mulberry tree. The berries were so red and so sweet. Was it wrong? How can it be wrong? *(He lets go of Hamid's shirt, sinking back down on the pillows.)*

Hamid: It wasn't wrong Dad….

Old man: *(He smiles.)* It was the most wondrous thing. Something that wonderful can never be wrong! It all happened during the revolution, but we were found out and punished . . . Khomeini was in power by then, I was flogged…. *(He clings onto Hamid's shoulder.)* But worse! A few weeks later some men threw acid in her face, it was all burnt away! She had no lips anymore, lips that were once sweet and red. *(He gently touches Hamid's lips.)* Just think Hamid! Can you picture that? *(He sits up again holding on to Hamid's shirt.)* Your mother was shamed, everyone knew, that's the real reason why we had to leave. You see this girl lived on the same street as us, after it happened, after her face was ruined I couldn't stay. Was I bad? Was it my fault?

Hamid: No Dad, it was never your fault, shit just happens….

Old man: You see I never really loved your mother, I didn't choose her, she didn't choose me. If I had the chance I'd lie under the mulberry tree with that beautiful girl again and again, I don't care how high the price is! Why does there have to be a price? Don't you see? *(He grips Hamid's shirt closer to him.)* It was their fault! They made us pay! All these years I've been sick with guilt . . . but I'm not guilty am I?

Hamid: You were never guilty Dad!

Old man: I know, it was them! They did it, they make the crime and they make the punishment. I want to live in a free world where you don't have to pay. *(He falls back on the pillows.)* And that's the truth and now you know!

Hamid: You told us the scars on your back were from the war.

Old man: They are war scars, just a different war.

Abbas, Faruzeh and Hosro come into the bedroom. Abbas has a bottle of whisky and a glass.

Hamid: Dad, look Abbas has brought you the whisky, do you still want some?

Old man: Of course! And fill the glass, fill it to the brim, let it overflow, it will be my last.

Abbas fills the glass to overflowing and passes it to Hamid who gently holds it to the old man's lips. He lifts his head and drinks it down greedily like a baby sucking milk from a teat. He drains it all and falls back on his pillows. Slowly Abbas, Faruzeh and Hosro gather together on the other side of the bed.

Old man: Ahh! That feels so good! I always thought I could beat the evil out of me, but it never worked, look at me now. Ha ha! *(He coughs.)*

Hamid: You were never evil Dad. *(He takes the old man's hand.)*

Old man: *(He pulls himself up, eyes wide open.)* But will I go to heaven or hell?

Hamid: Heaven!

Faruzeh: Heaven.

Abbas: You'll go to heaven.

Hosro: Of course you'll go to heaven Baba!

Old man: *(He sinks back down on the pillows, relieved, he sighs deeply.)* Tell me about heaven, what will heaven be like? Is it true what they say?

Hamid: There will be rivers of wine that will be delicious to those that drink. Bunches of fruit will hang low within your reach. Vessels of silver and cups of crystal will be passed around. You will be served by young boys as handsome as pearls. You will wear the finest silk clothing and sit upon a throne made of gold and decorated with precious stones.

Old man: And the Virgin Angels? The Houris?

Hamid: Heaven is full of them!

Old man: Just tell me about the Houris. *(He shuts his eyes, smiling.)*

Hamid: In the gardens of heaven will be virgins of modest gaze, reclining on couches of happiness arranged in rows, their faces as bright as the shining stars in heaven. Like red wine in a white glass, with large, round, pointed breasts that are high and never dangle. They never pee nor poo, they have no hairy legs and armpits just long luxurious hair and eyebrows like swallows wings. They never sweat nor smell bad and they never menstruate or bear children. A Houri does not want your wife to annoy you during your life on earth, as the Houri will be your wife when you go to heaven.

Old man: I think I'm going, I can feel it! . . . Wait! *(He opens his eyes lifting his head and points at Abbas who is crying and wiping his eyes with his sleeves.)* You bugger off! I don't want you going Hee Haw like a bloody donkey! Tsk! *(Abbas gets up, blowing his nose, he creeps from the room.)* Hosro?

Hosro: Yes Baba?

Old man: Look after Cyrus, promise me you'll take care of him. I have been looking into the numerology and it is no coincidence that God is Dog backwards! *(He* *lies back down.)* Now silence! I will begin my ascent to heaven.

The old man sees her. She slowly pulls off her burqa laying it on the bed. Underneath she's wearing a white nurses uniform and white shoes. Her skin is ivory white glowing like a pearl. Her long silvery tresses curl and float around her smooth sloping shoulders. She's beautiful, with red lips and red painted fingernails. She has gold angel wings strapped to her back made from the feathers of the bird of paradise and instead of a nurses cap she's wearing a clip on gold halo. She crooks her finger at him and beckons him towards her. She unzips the front of her dress revealing her pearly white breasts swelling from a white bra with silver tassels. From behind her she pulls out a bottle of red wine, she uncorks it with a pop and begins to laugh. She tips her head back and pours wine in her mouth and over her breasts and then leans forward proffering the bottle to the old man. She's the Houri, ever ready, ever willing. She will take him to paradise where the rivers will flow with wine and honey. She looks down at the old man smiling, and then picks up her burqa and throws it into the air letting it float down to cover the old man's head.

The Burqa Master Theatre Play

Introduction

The theatre play is in one act with ten scenes. The storyline is similar to the novel play, but I have excluded certain characters and plots to allow for one simple stage set that will accommodate the entire play.

Notes for the set

The set represents in a non-realistic fashion a sparsely furnished flat. The stage is split to represent two rooms. On the Stage Left is the 'Sitting room' with a dining table, a sofa and a TV. Downstage Left, behind the dining table is a shelf unit for crockery and miscellaneous items, including books, framed photos, telephone, calculator, pens and paper. Upstage Left is a window, which can be opened; net curtains hang down in front. There is a sitting room door on the Centre Left (Used for entering the sitting room and giving the idea it leads off to a corridor or other rooms in the flat.) Next to the door is a coat stand.

On the Stage Right is the 'Bedroom' with a double bed, a bedside lamp, a chair and dressing table. The top drawer contains syringes, scissors, comb, hairbrush, tie and a shaving mirror. The lower drawers contain old clothes.

On the Centre Right next to the bed is a clothes horse. A translucent screen is placed between Upstage Centre and Centre Stage partially separating the bedroom area from the living area. The screen has a simple open door frame in the centre, which the actors use to pass from one side to the other; giving the idea that the 2 rooms are separated by a wall. (This screen can be omitted.)

The action of the play takes place in two different flats. The change of flat can be brought about by changing the bedspread, sofa cover and the lighting. (Plus shelf items and miscellaneous props.)

The Babai Flat is lit with bright neon light and there is an oriental bedspread, oriental sofa cover and a large prayer mat on the floor. A cassette player (Sometimes on top of the TV, sometimes on the table.) There is a huge chandelier hanging above the prayer mat. (The chandelier must be raised when changing the scene to the Mohamed Flat.)

The Mohamed Flat has soft lighting. The bedspread and sofa cover are floral. There are perfumes, make-up and a hand mirror on the dressing table and a bedside table lamp with a red shade.

A small dog's settee is needed from Scene 6 onwards. Audio recordings: Door bell, Alarm clock, Muezzin chant, English lesson in Hamid's falsetto voice, Breaking glass, Loud banging/kicking on door, Door opening in corridor, Front door lock opening, Dog whine, Arabic pop music.

To speed up the scene-to-scene transitions; use stage lights down at the end of scene, and lights up at the start of new scene. (Unless curtain is indicated.) To make this appear natural, a prop light switch is used by the actors at the entrance to the sitting room door and a lamp in the bedroom, to coincide with lights up and lights down.

CHARACTERS OF THE PLAY

Behdad Babai (old man)
Hamid Babai (son)
Faruzeh (daughter)
Abbas (son-in-law)
Hosro- (grandson)
Jamshid Mohamed
Zina Mohamed
Neighbour (at Jamshid's flat)
Mr Akbar
Mummy Akbar
Hafsa Akbar
Fatima Akbar
Uncle Aziz
Turpin-Cyrus (small dog)

The dog should be a real dog. (A Jack Russell or about the same size.) The dog does not need to do anything, other than sit still and eat biscuits when given.
The dog on entering or exiting the stage is always carried and placed on a bed, a sofa or on the floor.
Therefore if it's impossible to have a 'real dog' a prop/fake dog could be used in its place.

ACT 1

Scene 1

(Curtain rises in darkness. Loud muezzin chanting is heard. Lights come up slowly revealing the two rooms of the Babai Flat. On the stage right the bedroom is empty. There is a partial screen with a doorway separating the two rooms. On the stage left is the sitting room. Two men are praying on the floor, an old man in a grubby tunic and his grandson Hosro in pyjamas. The old man's son, Hamid, sits at the dining table eating and watching them while they pray; he's dressed in jeans and a T-shirt. After several bows Hosro gets up and walks out the sitting room door on stage left.
The cassette player on the dining table clicks off abruptly in mid cry and the old man is suspended in mid undulation. He crawls across the carpet on his hands and knees and pulls himself to his feet by grabbing hold of the table. He picks up the huge cassette player and starts shaking it, then he bangs it down and pulls out the tape which has unravelled.)

Old man: *(Looking at Hamid.)* Finished already?
　　Stuffing your face! Where's Hosro?
Hamid: Gone back to bed if he's got any sense.

Old man: Any sense? Like his parents still in bed sleeping, it's a shame! *(The old man goes to the door. Hamid pours a second cup of coffee.)* Get up you lazy pigs! *(Shouting into corridor.)* Too lazy to pray! Too lazy to give your son his breakfast!

Hamid: *(Calling to his father from the table.)* DAD! It's only half past six. DAD!

Old man: *(Walking back to Hamid.)* Half past six! Then the corner store is open, go and get me the newspaper and ask that thick thicko Salim if my magazine has arrived.

Hamid: You only ordered it yesterday! *(Hamid puts on his leather jacket and starts to leave.)*

Old man: *(Calling after him.)* So what? And bring home a tin of Okho Chi and some boxes of Gaz. I want the ones that have the picture of the owner on the lid.

(The old man is left alone. He turns and sits down at the table and tries mending his cassette. His daughter Faruzeh and son-in-law Abbas enter the room. They are both dressed in jeans and Abbas is wearing a Kimono jacket with his longish hair tied in a ponytail. The old man stands up and looks at him in disgust.)

Abbas: Ahh! Is there any coffee left in the pot? *(He shakes the pot, gets a cup from the shelf and pours himself some coffee. He takes a biscuit from the plate on the table and munches.)*

Old man: What a cheek! Look at you filling your guts! Where were you?

Faruzeh: We prayed in the bedroom. Look, can you get Hosro up at eight or I'll be late to open the shop.

Old man: Why can't his father get him up? *(Pointing at Abbas.)*

Faruzeh: Abbas is dropping me off at work and he's on early shifts this week. *(Abbas, his mouth full of*

134

biscuits, nods and grunts in agreement.) We'll be
late....

*(She and Abbas put their coats on and head out the
door.)*

Old man: *(Sitting back down and picking up his
cassette, he starts unravelling the tape in a temper.)*
Bloody idiot, praying in the bedroom my arse!

*(The door bangs open and Hamid enters carrying a Jack
Russell dog in his arms.)*

Old man: *(Jumping up.)* What is this? Put it down and
kick it out the door, then wash your shoe seven
times. Oh my God you must wash all seven times!
Hands, jacket, everything! You halfwit! How many
times have I told you? Never touch a dog; you must
get rid of it!

Hamid: *(Kicking the door shut behind him.)* Dad listen,
I can't . . . I've saved him! Some bastard abandoned
him. He was tied to a lamp post outside the corner
store.

Old Man: I don't care what some other bloody bastard
did! You are not bringing a dog in the house. Oh
no! You tried many times as a boy and now you
think I am old and gaga? OUT WITH IT!

Hamid: I can't Dad, he won't do any harm.

Old man: Everyone knows Angel Gabriel will not enter
any home with a dog inside!

Hamid: Angel Gabriel doesn't visit us, even if we don't
have a dog!

Old man: How do you know what the Angel Gabriel
does? Dogs can't be in the house or he won't enter
and that's the truth! What is all this rescuing and
saving dogs? What is wrong with your brains?
(Snaps his fingers in front of Hamid's eyes.)

Hamid: Listen, I can't take him to the Dogs Home. Salim told me if they can't re-home him he'll be put down.

Old man: What does thicko Salim know about it? He can't even run the corner store!

Hamid: He has a sister who lives next to the Battersea Dogs Home! Anyway I had to adopt him, he's a great dog . . . he'll make a great pet.

Old man: You can't keep it as a pet because that's the custom of the bloody Kafirs and what is this adoption rubbish? Adopt a dog? Nonsense! Is he a human orphan? There's no reason to keep a dog as a pet it's a waste of time!

Hamid: Why not? What's wrong with him? Look at him! I've named him Turpin after the famous highwayman.

(The old man takes a quick glance at the dog cuddled up in Hamid's arms.)

Old man: It is not permissible for a Muslim to keep a dog. If people are praying and a dog walks within a stones throw of them, their prayer is made null and void. Listen Birdbrain! You can only have a dog if you are blind or deaf. Who ever keeps a dog loses the rewards for his good deeds! *(Turpin lets out a pitiful howl.)* Unless of course the dog is used for guarding a farm or cattle.

Hamid: That's it! We need a guard dog, rising crime in the area and all that, he'll be useful. *(Hamid holds the dog out to the old man who recoils backwards.)*

Old man: Don't talk rot! Look at him! A guard dog my arse! He's no bigger than a cat!

Hamid: He'll grow! He's intelligent. He'll bark if robbers try and break in!

Old man: At least he's not black, black dogs are evil! The devil in animal form.... All black dogs must be killed, they are Satan.... Hmm, he has a black patch over his eye . . . bad sign!

Hamid: Kill Scooby Doo? Kill Lassie?

Old man: Of course not! *(Throwing up his arms.)* Are you blind? I have seen Lassie myself on the telly and that silly Scooby Doo, and they are not black!

(Hosro enters; he's dressed in his school uniform.)

Hosro: WOW! A dog, where'd you find him? *(He reaches out to stroke the dog.)*

Old man: Don't touch it, come away! Come to the kitchen and I'll get your breakfast. *(The old man pulls Hosro by his jacket sleeve out through the door with him.)*

Hamid: *(He puts the dog down and takes a biscuit from the table.)* Here boy! *(He throws him the biscuit and the dog gobbles it up.)* Oh, hungry eh? You might as well have the lot! *(He puts the plate of biscuits down on the floor by the table and sits on the sofa watching the dog with a soppy grin on his face. Then his mobile phone rings.)* Hello.... Yes this is Reza Mahammed Al Haj.... Do you wish to speak to my widowed mother about English lessons? . . . Yes I will call her to the phone. *(Hamid stands up and puts the phone down on the table. He makes a quick shuffling tap dance and picks the phone back up. He then speaks in a high-pitched falsetto voice.)* Good morning! May I help you? *(He purses up his lips and flutters his eyelashes.)* Does your wife speak any English? *(He nods his head wisely then raises his eyebrows.)* Oh yes, I believe in full immersion, most definitely! I never speak in Persian, unless it's absolutely necessary.... Apart from general grammar and learning our ABC, I also teach passages from the classics, Shakespeare, Milton and so on.... Yes, it improves the vocabulary and diction. *(Pause, shaking his head.)* Considering my social position the lessons are absolutely private, I prefer to teach undisturbed.... Ah ha! *(Eyes upward, he simpers and pats into place his imaginary hairdo.)* I'm free on Tuesday and Thursday afternoons and charge 15 pounds per lesson. *(He narrows his eyes and smiles.)* Tuesday? Fine, could you give me your address? *(He scribbles it down.)* Yes, thank you, four O clock, Good-bye. *(Hamid puts the phone in his pocket, picks up the dog and leaves the sitting room.)* *(The light slowly darkens on stage to black.)*

ACT 1

Scene 2

(Lights up revealing the Babai flat in semi-darkness. Hosro comes through the door turning on the light switch and the sitting room floods with bright light. He's followed by Abbas and Faruzeh carrying trays loaded with food, which they set down on the dining table. Faruzeh is wearing an apron over her T-shirt and jeans. Abbas is wearing his favourite clothes, A Japanese silk kimono, Geta wooden Japanese flip flops on high wooden blocks, his long hair is drenched in oil and tied up in a samurai topknot. Abbas takes plates and glasses from the shelf and starts laying the table.)

Faruzeh: Hurry up I told them dinner at eight! *(Hosro starts picking at the food, she turns to him.)* Take off that school uniform, you have to leave soon.

Hosro: Do I have to go to the mosque with Baba? Please?

Faruzeh: Yes! It's all arranged, he's waiting there for you.

Hosro: It's not fair please can't you tell him I'm sick. I'll stay in my room I promise I won't bother you.... Oh go on?

Abbas: I don't see why he can't stay here?

Faruzeh: *(Exasperated.)* If he doesn't take Hosro for evening prayers, he'll stay home praying on the floor here in the middle of dinner.

Abbas: Please Hosro? Look, I'll give you extra pocket money to spend with your friends on Saturday.

Hosro: OK. *(Big sigh, he ambles out the door grabbing a handful of nuts off the table as he goes.)*

(Faruzeh begins folding paper serviettes into fans and putting them into the glasses. Abbas puts a tape in the cassette player of Arab pop songs with the volume low. The doorbell rings, Faruzeh takes off her apron and goes out the door. She returns with Sepideh and Sadam. Sadam plonks two bottles of wine on the table.)

Sadam: I see we have the house to ourselves!

(They kiss each other on the cheeks and sit down to eat, passing the dishes between them.)

Sadam: *(Uncorking the wine and filling their glasses. He holds his own full glass up in the air.)* Here's to us! By the way what have you done with the old man?

Faruzeh: Ohh.... He's at the mosque with Hosro.

Abbas: I wish he'd fucking go and live there! *(Picks up his glass of wine and drains it in one gulp.)* He's getting worse by the day, I can't stand it! Those prayers every bloody morning, he's even kicked a hole in the bedroom door.

Faruzeh: He hasn't, it's just dented.

Abbas: How many times have I trodden on his insulin syringes in my bare feet? I ask you? *(He stands up away from the table.)* I sat on one too the other day, I got the needle stuck in my arse, it snapped and I had to go to Casualty. *(He throws up his hands.)* Just think! I had to wait three hours because they said it wasn't an emergency, and I couldn't even sit down.

(They all laugh while Abbas dances, snapping his fingers in the air, stamping a loud rhythm to the Arab pop music. He dances over to Faruzeh and sits on her lap, she passes him another glass of wine and he drinks it all.)

Sepideh: Have you heard that Sharin's son is having an affair with a divorced woman, he's only sixteen!

Abbas: I can't believe it, how old is she?

Sepideh: About forty I'd say.

Faruzeh: And can't his mother stop him?

140

Sepideh: She's tried everything, she stopped his pocket money, and then he moved out, and now he's living with her.

Abbas: Hooey! She must be old enough to be . . . *(Strangled voice.)* his mother. *(He stands up.)*

(The old man has walked straight into the sitting room followed by a sheepish Hosro. The table freezes and conversation stops. The old man strides over to the window, he doesn't notice the dinner.)

Old man: The boy wanted to come home, says he feels sick.... It's stuffy in here, the air is no good! *(Shakes his head.)* No good air is bad for the brain.

(While the old man is opening the window Abbas whips up the wine bottles. He goes to the wall shelf and quickly hides the bottles behind a photograph of a holy man. He's in such a fluster he puts the photograph back upside down.)

Faruzeh: Hosro?

Hosro: I can't help it if I feel sick. *(He looks ashamed and guilty.)* I'm going to bed.

Old man: *(Turning to Hosro.)* Bring my insulin I need a shot!

(Hosro goes out the sitting room door. Faruzeh is panic-stricken and she sinks down in her chair. Abbas sits down too, looking worried.)

Abbas: Do you remember Sadam? And Sepideh?

Sadam: Good evening Sir.

(The old man steps over to the table, he peers closely at Sadam.)

Old man: Yes, my pleasure. *(Pointing his finger at Sadam.)* You're the one that married that fatty beautiful girl.

(Sadam stands up offering his hand. Sepideh stays in her seat.)

Old man: *(Ignoring Sadam, leaning forward, looking hard at Sepideh.)* Ehh, your husband not with you? *(Meanwhile Hosro has come back in, he's waiting with the syringe and insulin behind the old man, he coughs.)*

Old man: *(Turning round.)* Oh there you are!

(The old man sits down on the sofa, pulls his tunic up over his knee, prepares his syringe and jabs his thigh. The two guests are watching while Faruzeh and Abbas try not to notice and Hosro leaves the sitting room to go to bed.)

Old man: *(He stands up and throws the syringe on the sofa.)* Well, I never got the chance to finish my Isha prayers, Abbas, Sadam let us pray!

Abbas: We're eating.

Sadam: Erh, yeah, maybe after we've finished Sir.

Old man: Greed will be your downfall! *(He turns his back to them, and stands on his prayer mat reciting verses under his breath bowing up and down.)*

Abbas: This tart is delicious.

Faruzeh: Yes, I picked it up from the new bakery next to the shop. I had a hard time choosing.

Sepideh: Have you heard they're opening an ice skating rink at the park?

Abbas: Ice rink? It's not winter yet.

Sepideh: It'll be all year round, refrigerated under a dome.

Old man: *(The old man gets up and comes over to the table, he picks up some tart and shoves it in his mouth and starts talking with his mouth full.)* Refrigerated! What a waste of money, tsk, it will be a failure. *(He shakes his head sadly.)* Who'll want to go? *(He shrugs his shoulders.)* Now! *(He jabs his finger at them, then takes a chair and sits down.)* I've been thinking of a plan! A good business, do you know what? A laundry service! Buy some

142

washing machines and some irons and you know with a small investment we could make a lot of business.... Tsk.... Everybody has dirty washing! Women work, who has time to wash? Huh? *(He stuffs more tart in his mouth.)* Now I've been looking into this laundry business, it's a good thing. Get some machines and then you start.

Abbas: *(Sarcastic.)* Of course, how stupid I am! Why on earth didn't I think of it?

Old man: Because you're a fool, born a fool and will always be a fool. Ha ha, it's clear we only need to look at you! *(Suddenly taking in how Abbas is actually dressed.)* And what is that you are wearing tonight? *(He stands up and points at Abbas, his voice rising.)* A lady's dressing gown? What are those wooden contraptions you have upon your feet? Oh my God, what is this? Has my idiot daughter married a sissy boy, a pansy? Ooh, don't look shocked, the truth is always the truth.

Faruzeh: Dad, that's enough, finish your prayers!

Old man: *(Slams his fist down on the table.)* Finish my prayers? Who are you to tell me what I must do? What do you know of Qiyaam al-Layl? If a man is tired from long standing and recitation, he may allow some rest. True believers forsake their beds at night to invoke their lord in fear and hope and you! *(Points his finger at Abbas.)* He who sleeps all night gets up ill natured and lazy!

Abbas: I've become a Buddhist and follow the eightfold path! You're the one who gets up ill natured and lazy.

Old man: You filthy blaguard, what is this Buddhist rot? You were born a Muslim and will always be Muslim, so shut your bloody mouth and stop blaspheming. Who do you think you are? Are you Chinese? I dare say your guts are fat enough to be a Buddha. *(He walks away from the table and turns back to face Abbas.)* You want to kill me? How much shame must I carry on my shoulders? You are a donkey that's why you think you're a Buddhist. A Muslim should never give the Quran to a Buddhist. They mistake it for a comic book with a Mickey Mouse character called Mohammed in it. You're an imbecile just like them!

Sadam: Mr Babai, Sir, Buddha never professed himself a god, so what's the harm?

Old man: Don't you stick your big nose in my family affairs, you are here without your wife and she *(Points to Sepideh.)* is here without her husband. You can't pull the wool over my eyes. I know what's going on, in my own house too! *(Points to Faruzeh.)* It's a bad day when an old man comes home from the mosque, he wishes to pray and his prayers are drowned with talk of tarts. Am I disturbing your fine dinner party? Why wasn't I invited? Not even your own son! Why do you arrange all this without your family? *(He looks down under the table and kicks a plate across the floor.)* And how many times have I told you not to feed the bloody dog on our PLATES!

(The old man storms off through the screen doorway into his bedroom. He turns on the lamp. The bedroom lights up. The others continue eating in silence. Abbas gets up from the table and turns up the pop music very loud.)

Faruzeh: *(Shouting.)* Abbas, turn it down!

Abbas: *(Shouting.)* No! He's ruined my evening, I'll ruin his sleep! *(He starts to pile up the plates. The others help him and they clear the dining table taking everything out through the door to the kitchen.)*

(In his room the old man begins to undress, taking off his jacket and tunic, standing in his long underpants, his back is criss-crossed with scars. He pulls his long nightshirt over his head and gets into bed, turning off the bedside lamp. The bedroom darkens.)

Abbas: *(Enters the sitting room alone and wipes down the dining table with a cloth.)* Bugger him!

(Abbas turns off the cassette player and leaves turning out the light switch near the door. The sitting room darkens.)

(The stage darkens to black.)

ACT 1

Scene 3

(The stage lights up very slowly with an orange tint indicating sunrise. The old man's alarm clock rings loudly. He gets out of bed, walks into the sitting room and looks around suspiciously. He goes to the cassette player and takes out the tape throwing it across the floor. Then he gets a tape from the shelf, puts it in and presses play. Muezzin chants are playing full blast. He hurries out the sitting room door. Hosro comes into the sitting room in his pyjamas with a plate of toast and a mug of tea and puts them on the table. He goes back out again and comes in carrying the dog and sits him on the floor next to his chair.
The old man comes back in, drying his head with a towel and he lowers the volume on the cassette player. He begins bowing and praying on the carpet. Hosro is eating his breakfast and throwing toast crusts to the dog who gobbles them up.)

Old man: *(In mid-undulation he sees Hosro feeding the dog and stands up.)* Down Turpin! Hosro, dog's saliva is dirty so you can't let it lick you or get its wet fur on your clothes. The animal is a nitwit.

Hosro: Oh Grandad, look at him!

Old man: Better than a Hoover! But did you know a little puppy stopped an angel from entering the house because it was unclean? And if you touch a dog you must wash seven times. It is wrong! This Turpin he's a rascal and a bad influence, we should take him to Battersea Dogs Home!

Hosro: Look Baba you're upsetting his feelings!

146

Old man: Upsetting him my arse! No one listens to me, so how can a dog listen? It has no brains.

(Hosro gets up and takes his breakfast plate out to the kitchen. The old man starts walking round the sitting room muttering prayers and counting his prayer beads through his fingers. Hamid comes in with his breakfast on a tray and turns the cassette player off.)

Hamid: You've finished praying, right?

Old man: Maybe I have and maybe I haven't! Do I have any choice?

(The old man gets an Islamic comic paper for children from the shelf and sits down at the table next to Hamid. He flicks through the comic and finds a half finished crossword puzzle.)

Old man: Ahh, I never finished this! *(He checks his answers, his pen poised in the air then he underlines a new clue.)* Three down, the number of times we pray each day. Ahh that's easy, F, I, V, E, OK! Next, Muslims must do this once in a lifetime? Hajj of course. Ha ha, not bad for my age!

Hamid: Oh come off it, that's a kids comic, even Hosro's too old for it now!

Old man: Rubbish, this is not a kid's comic.

Hamid: Then why's it called The Islamic Playground? And why does it have Islamic colouring activities and Islamic number puzzles?

Old man: I have never coloured in the pictures, and do not pooh-hooh the crosswords, guess this if you can! Where is the kaabah located?

Hamid: Mecca!

Old man: No, you fool! It's Makkah! Not Mecca, and you want to know why? I'll tell you, tsk tsk, due to increasing misuse of our holy city's name, such as Motor-Mecca, Mecca-Bingo and such like, Saudi Arabia has officially changed the spelling. At the mosque we are planning to protest against the chain of pornographic cinemas called Mecca-Movies.

Hamid: Why bother if it's now called Makkah?

Old man: You don't understand, Muslims have a duty to be vigilant against sacrilegious and blasphemous acts and anything that is disrespectful. We must be the watchdogs for the sake of Islam!

Hamid: Yeah, next time you go on a protest, you can take Turpin!

Old man: How dare you? You are getting as bad as that idiot brother-in-law of yours! Did you know Abbas thinks he's a Buddhist?

Hamid: He is a Buddhist and he's become a vegetarian.

Old man: Impossible, it is not allowed. It is written 'Whoever changes his religion, kill him!'

Hamid: So you want to kill Abbas now? Ha ha....

(Hamid is laughing at him, the old man is getting angry, and he slams his fist down on the table.)

Old man: It is a dishonour to our family and why not? Not I, but there are others! If they come to know, maybe we will find him stabbed to death in a dark street.

Hamid: He's not important enough for anyone to bother going after. He's a nobody from nowhere, he's safe enough.

Old man: That's what you think!

Hamid: I'm going to the corner store to get some bread and milk. I'll take Turpin with me. *(Hamid stands up.)*

Old man: How many times do I have to tell you this dog is not permitted! Take him for a walk and don't bring him back! *(Hamid puts on his jacket.)* Pass me the Quran.

Hamid: What do you want that for now? I thought you were doing your crossword. *(He takes the Quran from the shelf holding it in his hand.)*

Old man: I've told you before, tsk tsk, we can interpret the text of the Quran by using numerology. There are matters I need to consult. You must of course seek out the right verse, the one pertaining to the question. *(Points at Hamid.)* For example when your sister told me she wanted to wed Abbas, I consulted a passage about matrimony, and do you remember? From the frequency of certain words and the numbers assigned to those words I came to know that he was the worst possible suitor.

(Hamid shakes his head.)

Hamid: I remember you telling us fortune telling was haram.

Old man: Nonsense, numerology is a science, give it to me, there are things I need to know.

(Hamid passes him the Quran and then picks up the dog and leaves the sitting room. The old man flicks through the pages before finding a suitable verse, he reads on jotting down his numbers, he feverishly starts adding them together.)

Old man: Holy . . . Master . . . Rumi? . . . Impossible! Abbas never! Aha! *(He looks up towards the photograph of the holy sage for inspiration, he sees it upside down.)* What?

(The old man jumps up and charges over to the shelf. He picks up the photograph to set it straight and then sees the bottles of wine hidden behind it. He pulls them out then looks to the ceiling.)

Old man: Thank you Allah, message received loud and clear. *(He sniffs the bottles.)* Devils, Devils....
(Mumbles, as he plonks the bottles on the dining table.) Aghh! A fool am I? Tsk.... A mule? *(The old*

149

*man rushes to the door and opens it shouting into
the corridor.)* Lazy devils! It's midday, lying in bed
in filth and drunken stupor! PIGS…. *(He hobbles
across the sitting room and enters his bedroom.
Fetching a large walking stick he goes back into the
sitting room and out through the door.)*

(Off Stage.) GET UP I TELL YOU! *(Loud banging, then
silence. He returns through the door carrying a
syringe.)* PAH! Useless, waste of time trying to wake
them!

*(He prepares the syringe at the dining table, then
steadying himself with his walking stick as though he's
suddenly become old and frail he goes over to sit down
on the sofa. He pulls up his tunic and injects himself. He
sits back and throws the empty syringe onto the floor. He
clasps his stick with both hands and closes his eyes, his
mouth opens slightly and he seems to be sleeping. There
is the sound of a bedroom door opening in the corridor,
then Faruzeh walks cautiously into the sitting room
followed by Abbas, they both look scared.)*

Abbas: Oh Shit…. He's still here! I thought he'd gone
out.

Faruzeh: *(Whining.)* I can't stop now. I have to meet
Sepideh at mid-day. I'm already late.

Abbas: Me neither, I have to go to work…. Why the
hell can't he mind his own fucking business? *(Sighs.)*

Faruzeh: Shit, shit! *(Pointing at the table.)* He found
the wine. *(Caresses the bottles.)* You forgot about
the bottles, remember? When he came home early
you hid them.

Abbas: Who cares? It's just an excuse to rage at us, at
me.

Faruzeh: Can't you talk to him? You've got time
before you leave. Just say sorry, calm him down a
bit.

Abbas: No way! *(Sulking.)*

Faruzeh: I can't face coming home tonight if you haven't had it out with him first. *(She touches Abbas's arm.)* It'll be worse later, best to get it over with right now…. *(She puts her head on one side like a cute bird.)* Please?

(Abbas goes over to the old man and kicks the syringe on the floor with his foot.)

Abbas: Look he's gone! Pathetic bastard. *(He leans into the old man's face.)* In the land of nod are you?

Faruzeh: Abbas, please? Look I've got to go. *(She turns and leaves.)* I'll call you later.

(Abbas stands still, staring at the old man, then he goes over to the stereo and puts on a cassette of Arab pop music turning the volume up loud. He bops around the old man for a while, and then he dances to the table where the wine bottles are and takes a swig from a bottle. He starts giggling. He puts the bottle down and dances back to the old man in the chair. Abbas spins on the spot like a mad dervish, every time he faces the old man he claps his hands like a gun shot right in the old man's face. Then he spins faster, clapping his hands above his head. He spins slowly, he shimmies his arse in the old mans face, he claps his fat red hands under the old man's nose, on and on his feet stamping the rhythm, wooden flip flops thumping the floor, his hands smarting from the stinging claps, he slaps his thighs, slap slap slap. The music slows down and he goes back to the table. He picks up the wine, shoves the bottleneck in his mouth, and glugs it down. He moves bopping back to stand in front of the old man, swigging on the bottle in small sips. He spills some wine down his chin and onto his white shirt, his face gets angry. He turns round and turns off the stereo, then he stands back in front of the old man.)

151

Abbas: Hey you old Bastard, wanna drink? *(He leans forward close to the old man's face.)* Go on! You cranky old fool…. Pah! *(He steps back.)* Look at you, no good for nothing, just sitting in your chair, shouting your mouth off and saying your prayers. You're ruining my life and why does my son call you Baba? I'm his bloody father! I'm sick of your bullshit, who do you think you are? … EH? … My son's father? Who am I eh? A childless donkey? Your fucking servant? *(Abbas holds out his hands in supplication still holding the bottle, voice whining.)* Oh Master, please I beg you, I implore you, can I scrub your floors? Can I empty your phlegm from the glass? Can I collect your yellow toenails off the mat? Please Master? AGGH OOHH….

(The old man brings his stick sharply up between Abbas's legs whacking him hard in the balls. Abbas staggers, falls on his knees and reels over backward, banging his head hard, he lays stunned on the carpet. The old man still sitting, stares into space, listening to Abbas groaning. He looks back down without expression watching Abbas struggling onto his hands and knees, coughing and spluttering. Hamid comes through the door with Turpin, singing a pop song.)

Hamid: Habibi Ha ha … Habibi Ha ha … Habibi … *(He stands in the doorway.)* I've got Turpin a new collar and lead! (*He steps into the sitting room carrying the dog, his mouth drops open when he sees Abbas down on the carpet.)* Dad? What have you done? *(The old man doesn't answer, he shrugs his shoulders.)* Dad, what's happened? DAD….

Old man: *(The old man stands up and pokes his stick at Abbas, whining like a child.)* It's his fault, not mine! He insulted me, called me a bastard…. Look he's

152

been drinking, in front of ME, he brought alcohol into the house. I wanted to complain about this. *(He waves his stick at the table where the other bottle is.)* He wouldn't come out of his room.

Hamid: I know Faruzeh phoned me.

Old man: I fell asleep . . . I'd taken my medicine. *(Points at Abbas.)* He woke me up! Shouting at me!

Hamid: Dad, you've got to slow down on the medicine. There are syringes all over the house. *(Old man looks up at the ceiling.)* Dad, please take it easy, huh? Don't be hard . . . Dad? *(Hamid puts Turpin down on the floor, picks up the fallen wine bottle and then he goes over to Abbas who is on his hands and knees still groaning. Hamid hauls him to his feet, shouldering him, they go out through the door.)*

Old man: *(Sitting back down.)* What's all this rubbish? *(He points at the dog.)* What is this new collar? Ugly, it doesn't suit you, yellow is sickly. *(He gets up and takes off the dog's collar and lead, throwing them on the sofa.)* And what a stupid name, 'Turpin.' Who ever heard of a dog named after some idiot highway robber? Now what we need is a name that suits, with the right number it will bring you some luck. *(He hobbles over to the shelf to fetch his calculator, pen and paper, and then he sits down at the table.)* Asad or Behrang? Now! *(He turns to Turpin.)* Every Arabic letter stands for a number, we call this Abjad. *(He totals and subtracts.)* Hmm? No, number one is not good for you! You see, it's the sun number and the rays of the sun will develop character such as arrogance and determination, very bad for a dog I think. *(He Looks at Turpin.)* Don't take it to heart I shall give you the perfect name. *(He taps away on his calculator.)* Peshman Babai? Parviz Babai? No! Bad numbers are two, six and

153

eight! These are the people who are full of problems and unsuccessful. *(More tapping.)* I have it, Cyrus! That is a name with a perfect number.... Now wait! *(The old man goes to the shelf, gets a tin of biscuits and puts them down on the floor in front of the dog.)* Hah! Now that's proper stuff, not scraps! You see? Your name is working for you already!

(While the dog eats the biscuits, the old man goes into his bedroom. He takes off his nightshirt showing the scars on his back. He puts on his tunic, jacket, sandals and a fez hat and then he goes into the sitting room. He puts the collar and lead back on the dog and they go out the door.)

(The stage lights dim slowly to darkness.)

ACT 1

Scene 4

(Lights up revealing the Babai flat in semi-darkness. Abbas enters and turns on the light switch. The sitting room lights up. Hosro follows him into the room.)

Abbas: *(He picks up the cassette player and turns round in a circle.)* I'm going to get my head down for a couple of hours; I had a long shift at work today.

Hosro: What are you doing?

Abbas: I'm going to hide this bloody ghetto blaster! No bloody muezzin calling me to prayers tonight.... *(He hides it behind the curtain.)*

Hosro: He'll find it there, it's too easy! Why don't you hang it by the handle out the window? There's a washing line hook under the window frame.

Abbas: Good thinking! *(He opens the window and hangs the cassette player outside.)* Ha ha, it's almost worth staying awake to see him look for it.... Ha ha....

(Abbas leaves the sitting room and Hosro turns on the TV settling down on the sofa to watch a cartoon. The old man comes into the room carrying a towel. He's wearing a tunic and is bare foot. He sits on a chair at the table and dries his feet.)

Old man: *(Stands up, throwing the towel over the chair back, he looks around.)* Where's the cassette player?

Hosro: Uhh! *(Pausing.)* Well, let me see Baba.... Where would you hide something, if you didn't want anyone to find it?

Old man: *(Going to the window, he opens it and lifts the cassette player back into the room putting it on the*

155

table.) Ha ha…. Your father thought he'd hide it from me, waste of time! He might as well have hung it from his big buckteeth! *(He hurries to the door and goes out into the corridor.)*

(Off stage.) Not even to atone yourself . . . After what you did! Curse the day I let you under my roof! PIG! Pray NOW or be DAMNED!

(Loud sound of a door being kicked over and over. Hosro turns off the TV and runs out the door. The kicking stops and the old man comes back into the sitting room. He hurries over to the cassette player and plays the muezzin chant tape at full volume. He stands on his carpet and begins to pray. Suddenly Abbas bursts through the door and stumbles against the table, he's followed by Hosro who remains in the doorway. Abbas is in his underpants, he charges over to the old man who is on his knees on the carpet and he kicks him in the butt making him fall flat on his face. He then races over to the cassette player, picks it up and throws it at the window curtains. There is a loud splintering sound of breaking glass. The cassette player falls down on the floor, the muezzin chant is still playing. The old man comes galloping up behind and throws himself on Abbas's back with his arms round his neck. Abbas sinks his teeth into the old man's arm biting hard. The old man lets go and seizes Abbas by his ponytail.)

Old man: Rabid dog! You bastard, you bit me!

(Abbas and the old man wrestle each other. The old man clings to his ponytail. Abbas elbows him in the gut and the old man collapses winded on the floor. The muezzin chant is still playing as Abbas returns to the window. He opens the curtain to one side and pulls open the cracked glass window, and chucks the cassette player out. Finally there is silence.)

Old man: You saw him! *(He turns to Hosro who is standing in the doorway shocked and bewildered.)* You saw what he did!

(He points wildly at Abbas, who just stands there, his eyes shining. The old man gets up off the floor stumbling and winded. He makes his way across the sitting room through the doorway into his bedroom, he turns on the bedside lamp. The bedroom lights up. The old man lies down on the bed.)

Hosro: Dad, you've cut your hand. I'll help you let's go to the bathroom. *(Abbas is just standing there dazed, he lets Hosro take his arm and lead him out the door.)*

(Curtain down.)

ACT 1

Scene 5

(Curtain rises in darkness. There's the sound of the TV with the volume set low. Lights come up slowly revealing the two rooms of the Mohamed Flat. In the sitting room Jamshid Mohamed is watching a TV programme in Persian. In the bedroom his wife Zina is sitting at the dressing table. She's making up her face and holding a hand mirror. She carefully applies her lipstick, and then she pouts and blows kisses to her reflection. The doorbell rings, she stands up and sprays herself with perfume.)

Jamshid: *(Jamshid gets up and opens the door, letting Hamid who's dressed in a full black burqa into the sitting room.)* Welcome, welcome please this way, wife is waiting. *(Hamid cannot be seen through his veil and he's wearing black gloves and white socks and sandals. He's carrying a bag and a small cassette player with him.)*

Jamshid: Erh! Madam, if you please remember last time you came I had no small change to pay, so I owe you for two lessons. *(Jamshid goes to the shelf, gets his wallet and takes out 30 pounds and hands it to Hamid.)*

Hamid: *(Falsetto.)* Thank you. *(He takes the cash and slips it in his pocket.)*

Jamshid: And how's my wife coming along? We are expecting big improvement! I forget, how many lessons you make so far?

Hamid: *(Falsetto.)* Oh about a dozen, she's doing well! She's a very good student.

Jamshid: Well, we are very happy! *(He shouts to the bedroom doorway.)* Zina! Your teacher is come!

(Jamshid stands aside and waves Hamid through the screen doorframe and returns to watch TV, lowering the volume a little. Hamid enters the bedroom throwing the bag on the bed. He puts the cassette player down on the dressing table and fiddles with the rewind and forward buttons. Jamshid creeps over to the screen wall with a glass, he presses the glass against the wall to listen.)

Hamid: *(Falsetto.)* Have you done your homework exercises Zina?

Zina: Yes, of course.

Hamid: *(Falsetto.)* Good girl you're one of my best students! *(He pats her bottom.)*

(Zina sits on the bed watching him. He presses play on the cassette player. The tape plays a very loud English lesson in Hamid's falsetto. 'I AM PLAYING, I WAS PLAYING, ARE YOU PLAYING? PLAY WITH ME! I AM SINGING, I WAS SINGING....' The tape continues repeating dull phrases. Jamshid stops listening, crosses the sitting room and goes out the door while the tape plays on. Hamid lifts off his veil and lifts up his burqa, underneath he's wearing red jockey shorts. With his skirt up he sits down on the chair and Zina straddles him. Hamid and Zina start snogging. Jamshid returns to the sitting room with a drink, he sits on the sofa with his feet up and changes the TV channels with his remote control. He's holds the drink on his stomach, while from the bedroom come the distinct sounds of Zina's lesson. 'IF I WERE RICH I'D BUY A PALACE, IF I WERE STRONG I'D HELP YOU LIFT YOUR SUITCASE, IF I WEREN'T RICH I COULDN'T BUY A PALACE, IF I WEREN'T STRONG I COULDN'T LIFT YOUR SUITCASE....' Zina unbuttons her blouse and Hamid dives inside with his hands. She's sitting astride him

159

wearing a pair of black zip boots and her red skirt is
rucked up round her thighs. She bounces energetically up
and down in Hamid's lap while he has his face
passionately buried inside her blouse. Jamshid is still in
the sitting room watching TV, then he gets up and
wanders out the door, returning with a packet of crisps.
He puts his feet up and opens the bag of crisps and eats
mechanically while watching TV, he drinks and burps,
picks his nose and scratches his arse. You can distinctly
hear the cassette player coming from the bedroom, now
reciting Paradise Lost. The doorbell rings, Jamshid gets
up, turns down the TV and opens the door. A middle-
aged man steps in through the doorway.)

Neighbour: Sorry to bother you but….

Jamshid: *(Interrupting him.)* NO! We don't want to
buy anything. Thank you. *(He starts to push him
out the door.)*

Neighbour: *(Trying to see over Jamshid's shoulder into
the sitting room.)* I'm your neighbour from
downstairs and I'm trying to do you a favour. See
this wallet! *(Holds out a wallet.)* Full of money, but
I'm honest right? So I'm bringing it to you!

Jamshid: *(Frowning and irritated.)* It's not mine. *(He
smiles sarcastically, he shakes his head and tries
again to push him out the door.)*

Neighbour: NO Wait! I was coming through the
hallway when I fell over a fat man in one of those
black cape jobs you Muslims wear. He were bent
down doing up his sandals. *(Jamshid shakes his
head.)* Everything fell out me shopping bag, I just
stuffed it all back in and I saw him go to your door.

Jamshid: Not into my house he didn't. That's enough!

Neighbour: He did! He rang your bell and put a black
shawl thingy on his head and it weren't till I got in
me flat and emptied me shopping I found his wallet.

So there you are! *(Jamshid's mouth gapes open, his eyes bulge.)*

Jamshid: The Bitch! *(Jamshid stands stock still, freezing for one moment, and then he snatches the wallet and opens it looking inside.)* The Bastard! Him! *(He grabs an umbrella from the coat stand and strides across the sitting room. The English lesson tape is still playing. Zina near to climax is bouncing feverishly up and down, still sitting astride Hamid. Jamshid charges in waving the umbrella.)* YOU FORGOT YOUR FUCKING WALLET! *(Throws wallet at Hamid.)*

(Then Jamshid leaps forward and starts beating both of them about the head and shoulders with his umbrella. The neighbour, unnoticed, has followed him to the bedroom and is watching through the doorway. Zina jumps up pulling her skirt down and holding her blouse together, screaming like a baby. Jamshid slaps Zina around the face, she screams louder and throws herself down on the bed.)

Zina: He make me do it…. I no want him…. *(Burying her face in her hands.)*

Jamshid: SHUT YOUR MOUTH! *(Hamid pulls his burqa down around him and spies his wallet fallen at Jamshid's feet. He looks at Jamshid, looks at Zina, then steps forward and makes a dive for it. Jamshid plunges the spike end of his umbrella in Hamid's shoulder.)* SON OF A DOG! PIMP! *(He beats Hamid on his back as Hamid scrambles for the door.)* MY DICK ON YOUR FOREHEAD! MY SHIT BETWEEN YOUR TEETH! *(Hamid runs out the bedroom crashing into the neighbour, stumbling through the sitting room to the door. Jamshid picks up Hamid's sandals and follows him.)* I SHIT ON YOUR FATHER'S GRAVE! I PISS ON YOUR

HEAD! *(Hamid runs out the door in his burqa and socks, Jamshid throws Hamid's sandals at his retreating back.)* YOU SON OF A SHOE!
(The English lesson is still playing 'IF I WERE A DOG I'D BRING YOUR SHOES, IF I WERE A CAT I'D CLIMB A TREE....')
(The light fades out fast, curtain down.)

ACT 1

Scene 6

(Curtain rises. Lights come up slowly revealing the two rooms of the Babai flat. The old man is sitting on the sofa wearing a long white grubby tunic. He's reading a newspaper and the dog is sitting on the floor next to him. Hosro is studying a physics textbook at the table and is writing equations in an exercise book.)

Hosro: Baba, can I use your calculator?

Old man: Getting stuck? HUH! You have to learn to concentrate, numbers, see here! *(The old man wobbles to his feet striding on his bandy legs to the shelf.)* Give me a number, any number, what's the root? Hah, I can tell you without a calculator. *(He gets a huge calculator down from the shelf, slides it across the table to Hosro and shifts stiffly back to the sofa.)* If your names on the wrong number.... Umm? You can make it into number five . . . and that'll cut off all these bad workings . . . and you'll get something someway.

Hosro: *(Smiles at the old man and puts on an interested face.)* Thanks Baba.

Old man: If your name is not agreed with you, you can have the name in number three. It will work for your prosperous.... And this is a very deep story, you have to WATCH when you change your name . . . you have to write it a hundred thousand times! Tsk! At least a hundred thousand times. Now back at home, we had a neighbour, she was a widow and only had one son. He was a fine boy, you know? Very tall, very honest and hardworking. Now when

163

it was time for him to marry, his mother chose him a wife, all the astrology was perfect, PERFECT! But it was no use. This girl, she was nasty to the mother, she wasted her husband's money down the toilet on perfumes and jewellery, and would not keep house because she was divooneh! Crazy! *(He taps the side of his head.)* All day at the cinema, no laundry, no cooking, nothing! So then he divorced her! After a year he married again, and this time his mother gave much money to the astrologist to get it right. They looked for a wife who would be diligent in the kitchen and you know what?

Hosro: *(Shakes his head.)* What?

Old man: This girl burnt down the kitchen and argued like the devil with everyone. She had a sharp tongue, better she had been born a dumb mule and so they were divorced. Then at last I said to the widow, 'We must change your son's name, there is nothing else to be done!' So after much calculation he was named Hooman, and I gave him some exercise books and he wrote his new name a hundred thousand times. I told his mother, 'Now you must find a girl by the name of Kobra, no other name will do.' It was all in the numbers you see? And you know what?

Hosro: *(Shrugs.)* What?

Old man: He married a fat beautiful girl and she was kind to his mother and generous with beggars, most of all she gave him nine children! Think of that, nine! Now nine is a very auspicious number too.... *(The doorbell rings, the old man gets up and shuffles to the doorway and goes out leaving the door open.)* *(Off stage.)* Bring it right up. *(Shouts at Hosro.)* The furniture has arrived! Help me carry it through!

164

(Hosro goes out the door, and then he and the old man carry a dog's miniature settee into the sitting room and arrange it next to the sofa.)

Hosro: Just like a real one!

Old man: *(Turning to the dog.)* Cyrus! Now you can see how your lucky name is working for you. Come on! Up!

(Hosro lifts the dog onto his own miniature faux black leather settee with leopard print cushions.)

Hosro: Look there's room for me too! *(Squeezing himself down next to the dog.)*

Old man: *(Plonking himself down on the sofa.)* Do you know I saw a film on the telly once? About a very rich old lady who had one of those sausage dogs, and it slept in a miniature four-poster bed. Ridiculous woman, what a fool! Hah hah.

Hosro: They probably only sell them in America!

(They watch the dog, say nothing but smile, then the doorbell rings again.)

Old man: Tsk, what have those delivery fools forgotten now? *(He goes back to the doorway and shouts.)* Salaam?

Jamshid: *(Off Stage, shouting.)* Does Hamid Babai live here?

Old man: He's not at home! Who is it?

Jamshid: Jamshid Mohamed, I have big serious complaint! Open up. *(Still shouting.)*

Old man: WAIT! *(The old man hobbles into the corridor and shuts the door behind him.)*

Hosro: Do you like your sofa Cyrus? Yes you do! *(He gently strokes the dog.)* Do you want a four-poster bed?

Old man: *(Coming back in through the door, followed by Jamshid.)* Hosro take your homework to your room and take Cyrus with you.

(Jamshid waits, looking disgusted as Hosro passes by him with the dog in his arms.)

Old man: Why have you come here? As you can see he's not at home, he's at the shop!

Jamshid: NO! He is not at your shop. You have no idea what he's up to! Did you know he has big advertisement poster in shop window? For a widow who is giving private lessons to Muslim housewives!

Old man: So what?

Jamshid: Only there is no widow, he's the widow disguised in a burqa! *(Jamshid pauses waiting for the old man's comprehension and outrage.)*

Old man: Nonsense!

Jamshid: *(Furious.)* It is true! He came…. *(Louder.)* He has been coming many weeks to MY house, for giving English lessons to MY wife! This widow is telling everyone she only giving lesson in private room. *(He shakes his head wildly, his wiry beard glistening with sprayed saliva.)* I AM BELIEVING HE IS A WOMAN! I AM SENDING HIM TO MY BEDROOM ALONE WITH MY WIFE! *(He slaps his forehead.)* Just think with my poor mother there! Who knows what scenes Maman has witnessed? The shame! He has defiled my home, dishonoured me…. *(His voice rises higher screeching.)* IT IS WORSE THAN DEATH! *(He freezes, his jaw drops open, then he hisses choking and spitting.)* He tricked money from me, I paid him!

Old man: *(Confused, backing away.)* Paid him?

Jamshid: For the lessons…. Do you not understand? We are all believing he is harmless old widow! *(The old man sits down shocked on the dog's settee.)* I know of other men in our community who have paid him for same set up! AND NOW! IN THE END! I DISCOVER THE DEVIL IN MY

166

BEDROOM! *(He shakes his head, his lips twisted in a sick smile.)* He ran away but I will find him! I will ruin him and your family, all of you! Who do you think will be coming to your shop after this? . . . Also much divorce! All will want him dead!

(There is silence. The two stare deeply at each other. Time stands still, while the old man's mind is working.)

Old man: *(He stands up looking right into Jamshid's eyes with a piercing gaze.)* What about your honour? Your son's honour? It is also bad for you if this becomes public.

Jamshid: *(His eyes narrow.)* I want punishment! Something must be done! *(Voice rising.)* Do you think I can sit and do nothing?

Old man: What do you want to do?

Jamshid: Sharia! *(His eyes shine with visions.)*

Old man: *(Whispers.)* Sharia? Here?

Jamshid: *(Waving his arms.)* We can organize in some back garden and justice will be done!

Old man: *(Shouting.)* Are you mad? We are here! This is the land of Kafirs! We cannot carry on as if we were back at home. *(Throwing his hands up in despair.)* Just look at the telly! *(Jabs his finger at the television. Jamshid spins round staring at the black screen.)* Men and women having affairs all over the place, in cars and offices and even in bloody toilets! And what are the consequences? I'll tell you! *(Stepping towards Jamshid.)* Nothing! Bloody nothing, no one has to pay, they do it, and that's the end of it!

Jamshid: *(Whining.)* There must be justice!

Old man: Justice? Hah! What is justice? What can I do? I can shout at him till I break his ears and I can beat him when I catch him asleep, otherwise he's too fast for my stick.... And that's it! That's the most I can do, and even that's illegal here! *(Points in Jamshid's* *face.)* Did you know that? He could denounce me to the police, and I would be arrested for beating my own son. They won't care if he's committed adultery, they all do it! I'll be in prison and he'll be free!

Jamshid: *(Sneering.)* So you're afraid to beat your own son!

Old man: Of course not! He'd never denounce his own father! But that's all I can do. You have no idea, every day I must swallow insults, you must learn to swallow the insults!

Jamshid: Never!

Old man: What else can you do? My daughter, does she wear a veil or even a scarf to cover her hair? No! She refuses and what must I do? Beat her? My son-in-law won't go to the Mosque! What must I do? Drag him there? *(Turns his back on Jamshid and walks towards the window, then he spins round fast, facing Jamshid again.)* Even my grandson has a pet dog!

Jamshid: But something you must do!

Old man: YES! I have three choices, grin and bear it, live alone or return to Iran! *(He steps right up to Jamshid, his eyes boring into his soul.)* Believe me, it's best you keep your mouth shut for the sake of your family, and that is the most you can do.

(Jamshid gives up. He walks slowly towards the door, and then turns round pointing at the old man.)

Jamshid: Shame on you! You are well known for being very religious, but today you give me no help, you are telling me to let them do want they want! I cannot believe it.

Old Man: Do you know what I pray for? No! Of course not, you know nothing about me! You don't know me at all.

168

Jamshid: At least you know what a no good filthy pig of a son you have!

Old man: I have always known it myself.

Jamshid: You should punish him! Throw him in the street . . . with nothing!

Old man: I should.

Jamshid: But will you?

Old man: *(Staring hard at Jamshid.)* Who can say?

(Jamshid leaves slamming the door behind him. The old man goes into his bedroom. He opens the dressing table drawers, and rummages through the clothes pulling them out and pushing them back in, then he slams the drawers shut. He sits on the edge of his bed, his head in his hands, and then he lies down on the bed.)

(The stage darkens to black.)

ACT 1

Scene 7

(Lights up revealing the Babai flat in semi-darkness. There's the clunking sound of the front door being unlocked. The old man sits up in bed and turns on the lamp. The bedroom lights up. He gets up and takes his walking stick, and then he stands in the bedroom doorway. Hamid appears in the sitting room doorway and turns on the light switch. The sitting room lights up. He shuts the door quietly. He's wearing a tight T-shirt that exposes his stomach and a green pair of women's leggings and rubber flip-flops. He has a black eye and is carrying a plastic shopping bag.)

Old man: THERE YOU ARE! *(He stands in the bedroom doorway, pointing his stick at Hamid.)* YOU SWINE! *(Breathless voice.)* I had a visitor today.... JAMSHID MOHAMMED! What the hell are you playing at?

Hamid: *(Hamid looks bewildered, like a son laying eyes on his father for the first time in years.)* I've been earning some extra cash teaching English, but I was brought down by a bad woman. *(Shocked by his own confession, he falls to his knees.)* Dad, I'm a useless sack of shit! To think I was brought down by a cruel woman who beats up her midget mother-in-law, sorry Dad.

Old man: SORRY! YOU'RE SORRY? *(He strides towards Hamid and pokes him with his walking stick.)* What do I care if she beats up midgets? Get your arse up!

(Hamid doesn't move. The old man jerks him to his feet by his T-shirt, and swipes Hamid in the guts with his stick. There's a loud crash as Hamid trips backwards knocking a dining table chair over.)

Old man: Give me that bag!

Hamid: Leave it Dad, it's just some stuff.

Old man: You think I'm a fool? Yes I am a fool! I searched through your dead mother's clothes and do you know what I found gone? No, STOLEN? *(Waving his arms and getting agitated.)* Guess what is missing?

Hamid: Dad it's late! *(The old man lunges for the bag.)* Let it alone....

(Abbas opens the sitting room door and stands in the doorway; he scrunches up his eyes against the thumping glare of neon light. Hamid and the old man are pouring sweat, fighting over the bag. The old man snatches it from him at last, and pulls out his wife's old black musty burqa.)

Old man: Where did you get? It's your mother's . . . ISN'T IT? . . . YOU SWINE!

Hamid: I borrowed it to teach English.

Old man: Teach my arse! *(He cackles.)* Take you out and shoot you, I say! Teach my arse!

(Faruzeh comes up behind Abbas and pushes past him into the sitting room, Abbas follows her. Hamid turns to make a dash for the door.)

Old man: COME BACK HERE!

(He hooks Hamid's shoulder with his walking stick and brings him down. Hamid scrambles to his feet, the old man lunges at him with the stick. Hamid grabs hold of the fallen chair and holds it up in front of him like a shield. The old man holding the burqa in one hand and his walking stick in the other, hits at the chair with his stick getting it stuck in the chair legs. Faruzeh and Abbas

watch transfixed as everything moves like an old film reel. The old man keeps bringing his stick down hard on the chair rim again and again, while Hamid struggles to hold his chair up in front. On and on he drives Hamid backwards across the sitting room. The chair slips crashing to the floor. The old man points his stick at Hamid's throat. Hamid falls to the floor rolling himself into a hedgehog, but the old man drops the burqa and grabs his hair yanking him, making him stand back up. Then the old man staggers sideways, stumbling over the fallen chair. He grabs Hamid's shoulder, gasping, as he can't get his breath.)

Hamid: DAD! DAD? *(Hamid tries to support his father but the old man pushes him away. He lets his stick drop to the floor and leans on the table, wheezing and gasping for breath.)* Dad, are you OK?

Old man: Faruzeh, get my insulin.

Faruzeh: Dad let me help you back to bed, Abbas will get it. *(Abbas goes out the door. She helps the old man across the sitting room into his bedroom, and pulls back the bed sheets helping him into bed.)* Here we go! *(She pulls off his slippers and tucks him in.)*

Abbas: *(He returns with the old man's syringe, and shakes his head at Hamid who is tidying up the sitting room.)* You need some ice for your eye!

Hamid: No it's OK…. I'd better go for a few days. If you need me I'll be at Patty's.

Abbas: I thought you and she had split up. *(Abbas scratches his stomach.)*

Hamid: Not really, it's off and on, and that's my fault too. I'm such an arsehole and she's an angel. She lent me these clothes earlier on, when I turned up at her place, barefoot with nothing but my burqa!

(Abbas pats Hamid's shoulder giving him a conspiratorial grimace and then goes into the bedroom.

Hamid picks up the shopping bag and the old burqa and walks out the door. Faruzeh takes the syringe from Abbas and gives her father a shot. Abbas stands watching with his hands in his pockets, then Faruzeh stands up and turns off the bedside lamp. The bedroom turns dark. Faruzeh and Abbas cross the sitting room and head out the door turning off the light. The sitting room turns dark.)
(The stage darkens to black.)

ACT 1

Scene 8

(The stage slowly lightens turning to daylight. The old man gets out of bed and creeps into the sitting room. He gets a tin of fudge and a newspaper from the shelf. He carries them back to his bedroom and starts getting into bed, then he stops and rushes back to the sitting room. He picks the dog up from the little settee and takes him into the bedroom too. He settles the dog down on the bed, and carefully gets back inside the covers. The old man starts reading the newspaper and eating fudge from the tin, his hand goes up and down mechanically from tin to mouth to tin, tossing fudge in his gob and chewing fast. The dog is sitting on the end of his bed and every now and then he tosses him a cube of fudge. Hamid comes into the sitting room. He's carrying a suitcase and a huge yellow cassette player tied with a red ribbon. He puts them down by the table and inspects the shelves. He removes some books and music cassettes putting them in the outside flap of his suitcase.)

Hamid: *(Shouting through doorway to the old man.)* Dad, I'm here! How are you? *(The old man takes no notice of him. Hamid puts the case near the door and takes the cassette player into the bedroom and puts it down by the doorway.)* Dad? I'm off now, I'll drop in after work on Monday . . . Dad, I'm off!

Old man: *(Putting down his newspaper.)* You're not OFF! Do not speak to me as though you are just going out and will be home later! You have not been home for over a week and I know you are living with that Kafir woman! You have left your home and never had the guts to say so!

Hamid: Dad, that's not fair, her name's Patty. *(He looks so guilty.)* Look would you like me to sleep here tonight?

Old man: NO! Don't bother, I don't need your pity! I'm sick and old . . . and alone. I'm an old man who has lost his own son! I never see you anymore.

Hamid: *(Resigned, he shakes his head.)* Dad, that's not true. I come home every day after I shut the shop....

Old man: *(Voice querulous and whining.)* It's not the same. You are living somewhere else. You don't even come back for morning prayers.... *(Hamid fusses around straightening the bedcovers, not wanting to meet his father's gaze.)* Do you know? I'd wake most nights, I still do, can't sleep. I used to come and watch you sleeping in your room, it made me feel comfy.

Hamid: *(Uncomfortable.)* You don't need to watch me sleeping Dad, you can watch Hosro now.

Old man: AGGH! He's changed. *(Old man jabs his finger in the air.)* Become sneaking he has, just like a serpent.... Now I sit in bed at night, and instead of hearing my son coming home at three in the morning, I hear my grandson lurking about, smoking and watching porno videos because he thinks I'm sleeping. Is that a life for me?

Hamid: Anyway you have Turpin and don't deny it Dad. Look at him! He's become as fat as a baby pig.

Old man: Don't talk rubbish, how many times do I have to tell you all? He's just a guard dog and his name's Cyrus. I need him in the room at night. I have been informed that dogs are famous for alerting their owners to gas leaks, fires, heart attacks

175

and the like, and at my age I need him as extra security.

Hamid: You didn't have to let him on the bed. He could sleep on the floor!

Old man: Just get on with your packing, leave if you must but you're not taking Cyrus with you.

Hamid: I don't want him!

Old man: He's the only one who listens to me! Just think of that! I have a family, but the only one I can talk to is a dog! And he's not even permitted! *(The old man goes back to reading his newspaper.)*

Hamid: I'll be in after work . . . every day, same as usual I promise. *(Softly.)* Look Dad, why don't you get a hobby?

Old man: Hobby my arse! Hobbies are for fools with nothing better to do.

(The old man turns his back on Hamid, rolling over upsetting the sweets on the bed. Hamid picks them up and puts them back in the tin on the dressing table. He pats the dog, then remembers the cassette player by the door and picks it up.)

Hamid: Dad, look I've bought you a present....

Old man: *(His back to Hamid.)* Don't want a bloody present. I'm not a child, I'm not bloody gaga yet!

Hamid: You don't know what it is! *(He presses play and muezzin chanting starts. The old man turns round sitting up. Hamid stops the cassette.)* I bought you a brand new tape too!

Old man: It's enormous, and it's bright yellow, bloody ridiculous!

Hamid: I can take it back and get you a smaller one....

Old man: I don't want you wasting time running backwards and forwards to the shops. I suppose I'll get used to it. How many decibels?

Hamid: A lot, it's the loudest they had in the store!

Old man: Put it under my bed, before that buffoon Abbas gets sight of it! *(He lies back down.)* I'm running low on sweets, Faruzeh has put me on rations. Bring me some extra tins of Okho Chi next time!

Hamid: OK, I'll see you on Monday. *(He pats the dog, then goes back through the sitting room, takes his suitcase and leaves.)*

(When the door in the sitting room shuts, the old man sits back up. He looks at the dog sitting at his feet on the end of the bed.)

Old man: Cyrus, you see what an ungrateful son I have! You were abandoned by your master, and I by my son! We both know what it is to nurse a viper in our bosom! And to think! I gave him the best name! Our prophet said, 'Give your child a good name.' And what did I do? I gave him the best, a name with number three, so is it my fault? No it cannot be! It is well known that some of these people with good numbers, like one, three and nine, still they are having problems, and why? The answer lies in the words of a renowned Islamic scholar. 'Bad marriage combinations can ruin a man for life! No matter what his name!' *(The dog whines softly. The old man leans forward patting the dog's head.)* You're right he's not even married, so it must be that Kafir woman he's having an affair with. He should marry. Of course! And we have to find a Muslim girl with the right number. I must not neglect my duties as head of the household, and all will come right in the end! Ha ha, maybe one for Hosro too?

(He swings his legs out of bed and hobbles into the sitting room. He gets an address book down from the shelf and the telephone. He sits down and starts thumbing through

the addresses, then he picks up the phone and dials holding the phone to his ear.)

Old man: Salaam! It is me Behdad.... Yes, a long time but I am coming to visit you today.... Of course I shall be happy to stay for lunch.... Ahh hah.... OK! I'm on my way.... *(He puts the phone back on the shelf and hurries to his bedroom. He takes his fez cap and jacket, and like a joyful child he kicks off his slippers making them fly high across the bedroom. He slides his feet into a pair of sandals and picks up the dog carrying him back to the settee in the sitting room.)* Now Cyrus, guard the house! *(He hurries out the door.)*

(The light slowly darkens until the stage is black.)

ACT 1

Scene 9

(Lights up revealing the Babai flat in semi-darkness. The door opens and Abbas turns on the light switch. The sitting room lights up. Abbas is carrying a tray with food and he starts to set the table with dishes and glasses from the shelf. Hosro comes through the door carrying a stack of kitchen chairs, which he puts in front of the TV, and then he goes to help Abbas set out the cutlery. The dog is on his settee. Hamid comes through the door and sits down on one of the kitchen chairs and lights a cigarette. Faruzeh walks in bringing a large platter of rice balls to the table.)

Hamid: Who are the others?

Faruzeh: I don't know! Some distant relatives? It's supposed to be a surprise.

(Hamid shakes his head slowly and draws deeply on his cigarette then he gets up and follows Faruzeh out the door.)

Old man: *(The old man comes charging through the door dressed in his best clothes.)* Hosro come with me! *(Hosro follows him to the bedroom. He turns on the lamp. The bedroom lights up. The old man extracts a silk striped tie from the dressing table drawer. He puts it round Hosro's neck making a tight knot. Hosro's hair is spiky with Brylcreem and he's looking resigned and sulky.)* That's no way to have a hairstyle, tsk, a freaks style, looks as if you've been electrocuted!

Hosro: And you'd know just how they look.

(The old man ignores him. He takes a big comb from the drawer and flattens down Hosro's hair with a side parting, he then hands him a magnified shaving mirror.)

Hosro: *(Hosro peers at himself.)* I'm not coming out like this! I look a real creep! *(Panic.)*

Old man: *(Laughs.)* You looked a bloody creep before! Now, shape up! Millions of people all around the world have ridiculous hairstyles, look at your father! But those who become bloody pop stars are rare, it's all a matter of fate. It's all in the bones, if you're born with the bones of a beggar, that's how you'll spend your life. *(The doorbell rings and the old man goes into the sitting room, leaving Hosro standing there.)*

(Faruzeh brings an old couple into the sitting room followed by two women. Mummy Akbar is fat and pyramid shaped and she's wearing a headscarf tied under her chin. Her husband, Mr Akbar, is a skinny old man with shiny medals pinned to his chest. He's wearing a tunic and jacket. The two young women are wearing identical red trouser suits, sporting the same beehive hairdo's with three ringlets hanging down each side framing their faces, they look like plaster window dummies. Fatima is sixteen years old, she's fat just like her mummy, with thick make up on her face and bright red lipstick, she keeps smiling. The niece Hafsa is over thirty, her long thin neck and face are covered in moles. Meanwhile, in the bedroom Hosro is spiking his hair up again.)

Mr Akbar: Hello my dear friend, as you see I've brought my good lady wife and the girls!

Old man: Salaam! *(He kisses Mr Akbar's cheeks.)* Welcome, come in and take a seat. *(The old couple sit at the table.)* No, you there! *(Hafsa goes to sit on the sofa next to her cousin Fatima, but he pushes*

180

Hafsa into a chair next to the TV.) Hosro! *(Shouting towards the bedroom, Hosro enters with his hair spiked up.)* Aghh, my grandson! *(He takes hold of Hosro's shoulder pushing him in front of the Akbars.)* Hosro's nearly seventeen, a fine young man, eh? *(He gestures towards the Akbars.)* You remember Mr Hussein Akbar? A cousin on Aunt Sepideh's side! This is his good lady and their daughter Fatima and their niece Hafsa.... *(He doesn't bother to turn towards Hafsa, in fact he's standing in front of her, blocking her from view.)*

Mr Akbar: *(Stands up and shakes Hosro's hand.)* Heeloo, *(In a sing song voice.)* My how you've grown, what? We haven't seen you since Babeck's wedding.... Five years ago, how time flies.... *(He continues pumping Hosro's hand shaking him to pieces.)*

Mummy Akbar: *(From her chair.)* Hello.

Fatima: Hello. *(The old man shoves Hosro down on the sofa next to Fatima.)*

Hafsa: Hello. *(From behind the old man.)*

(The old man takes a photo album from the shelf and drops it in Hosro's lap.)

Old man: Take a look at your cousins wedding photographs. *(Looking at the Akbars.)* Practically the same age you know, Hosro and his cousin. *(Looking down at Hosro.)* Shame your parents didn't take you!

Faruzeh: It was in Tehran during the school term.

Old man: Abdul went! *(Turning to the Akbars.)* Hosro is studying for his A levels, then off to study medicine or engineering. Huh? What do you have to say Hosro?

(Hosro is sitting staring ahead, his face red and shining. He opens the album and takes out a bunch of photos

*and begins to pass them around. The Akbars quietly coo
and cackle at the photos. Hamid enters with a large tray
of baklava and places it on the table.)*

Hamid: Home made! Faruzeh, can you cut it for me?
*(He hands her a large knife and she begins to cut the
baklava into cubes. The old man is standing smiling and
nodding, watching Hosro passing round the photos with
the Akbars.)*

Old man: Family photographs, nothing like it!
Weddings . . . I say you're never too young or old,
(Looking at Hamid.) . . . to get married.

Faruzeh: I want a word with you two. *(Pointing to
Abbas and Hamid. She collars them both and pulls
them into the old man's bedroom.)* I know what his
game is, that Fatima girl and her bloody parents!

Abbas: So what?

Faruzeh: So what? *(She huffs impatiently.)* Don't you
see what he's up to? He's interfering, trying to
marry Hosro.

Hamid: Huh, it's just a coincidence. *(He shrugs.)*
You're getting paranoid.

Faruzeh: You heard him Hamid! *(She mimics the old
man's voice.)* 'Cousin's wedding, they're the same
age!' Hosro's going to be a bloody doctor now! Or
was it engineer? Just listen to him!

*(In the sitting room Hosro is sitting rigidly on the sofa
staring at the photos. Hafsa is carefully picking her ear.
Fatima twiddles one of her ringlets around her finger,
sneaking looks at Hosro.)*

Old man: Tsk tsk! *(Peering closely at a photo.)* Well
there's a thing.... You just never can tell.

Akbars: Laugh in unison.

*(Hosro sees Fatima looking at him, she makes a sulky
moue at him and Hosro looks away. The old man gets
up.)*

182

Old man: One moment please.... *(He crosses the room into the bedroom, the others continue passing round the photos.)*

Mr Akbar: Well Hosro, and what have you to say about yourself.... We're waiting.... What? *(He cups his hand around his ear, the girls laugh.)*

Old man: *(Entering the bedroom.)* What are you doing sneaking around my bedroom? It's time to start eating.

Faruzeh: Don't you dare sit Hosro next to that Fatima girl!

Old man: And what's wrong with her? That girl is a nice good girl and her parents are related. It's time Hosro was introduced to some decent families. He must meet the right kind of girl, I have checked her numbers and astrology says yes!

Faruzeh: Are you mad? He's only sixteen! We are not living a hundred years ago.

Old man: Nonsense! There is no harm and I am the head of the family, I will decide!

Hamid: Dad's right, I think she looks lovely. She'll make a fine bride for Hosro. *(Abbas and Hamid double over laughing. The old man is furious.)*

Old man: *(He jabs angrily at Hamid.)* You! After the trouble you've made, better for you to get to know the niece, I have chosen her for you!

Hamid: Please Dad, not the chicken woman! *(Abbas hoots with laughter, Faruzeh giggles.)*

Old man: *(To Abbas.)* YOU! SHUT YOUR FACE! HOW DARE YOU.... *(He clutches the front of Abbas's shirt, half hanging on.)* You married MY daughter without MY permission. Do you think I'd have chosen an Ass like you?

(Meanwhile the Akbars have become aware of the shouting. They carry on sifting through the photos but

mummy Akbar gets up and creeps over to the bedroom doorway.)

Old man: Cretin! Moron! Nerd! Ninny! Simpleton! Clod! Dumbass! Dunce.... *(Abbas jerks his shirt from the old man's grasp pushing him backwards on the bed.)* Right! You want to have another fight? *(He pulls open the dressing table drawer.)* I haven't forgotten the cassette player fat boy! *(He pulls a large pair of scissors from the drawer.)* You're a long haired twit, you need a haircut. *(Snipping the scissors at Abbas who backs up towards the door.)* Ha ha! Like a schoolgirl with a stupid ponytail.... It needs chopping off!

(He charges at Abbas who ducks sideways as Mummy Akbar walks into the bedroom behind him. The old man stumbles forwards with the scissors in his hand, she screams, they collide, she falls backwards on the bedroom floor as the old man lands on top of her. The old man scrambles to his feet; out of breath he chucks the scissors on the bed.)

Old man: *(Facing Abbas.)* This is all your fault! *(He points to Mummy Akbar on the floor.)* Lucky for you she doesn't have a scratch on her!

(Hosro, Mr Akbar, and the girls jump up and rush into the bedroom. Hamid puts the scissors in the drawer while everyone else is staring at Mummy Akbar lying on the floor.)

Old man: Carry her to the couch! Carry her through! Just fainted, that's all.

Hafsa: What happened?

Old man: Maybe she's fainted from hunger, she just fell down when she walked in. Hamid you take her by the left! *(The old man lifts under her right arm.)* HOSRO LEGS!

184

(They struggle to lift her off the floor. They finally get a hold of her. Hosro has lifted her legs up, and to get the leverage he's standing squashed between them. Her skirt falls back and she's wearing stockings and suspenders.)

Mr Akbar: Get a grip! . . . HOLD TIGHT! *(He watches them lift her, while Faruzeh lies down on the old man's bed and Abbas sits next to her massaging her temples.)* Mind her now! *(The old man and Hamid have her under the armpits, they start swaying and straining, her bottom drags along the floor as they go through the doorway. In the sitting room they bash her really hard against the dining table.)* Be careful!

Fatima: Ooh her head! *(She clings on to Hafsa.)*

(They struggle across the room to the sofa. The old man gives out and lets go, she slips out of Hamid's grasp and with her legs still wrapped around Hosro's thighs her head drops on the floor.)

Mr Akbar: Careful now, nice and easy does it.

Fatima: AGHH! Mummy?

(The old man is bent over winded, while Hamid has staggered back and sat in a chair. The three Akbars are standing together watching. Hafsa has her arm around Fatima. Hosro is stooped over Mummy Akbar, still holding her legs he drops them on the sofa.)

Old man: *(Straightening up panting out of breath.)* That's right Hosro! Legs up, head down, perfect position to recover from a fainting fit. A cushion for her head…. *(He looks at the Akbars.)* Not to worry, to overcome a faint, the legs must be kept above the head. *(Mummy Akbar is lying twisted on the floor with her legs up on the sofa. The old man takes a cushion and pulls her head up by her headscarf and shoves the cushion underneath.)*

Fatima: MUMMY?

Hafsa: *(Still hugging Fatima to her.)* Uncle, don't you think we should call an ambulance?

Mr Akbar: *(Bewildered.)* Umm....

Old man: Nonsense! She'll come round soon enough. As I said, fainted when she walked in the bedroom, just needs a little rest. Well Hussein, shall we eat? Lots of delicious food sitting there waiting for us, what? *(Hosro stands still, while they slowly take their places and sit down to eat.)* HOSRO, come and eat!

(Everyone is eating in silence except the old man who eats with his mouth open and makes loud sucking sounds throughout the meal. Abbas leaves Faruzeh sulking on the old man's bed and crosses the sitting room going out through the door.)

Mr Akbar: Not coming to eat your son-in-law?

Old man: Can't he's got a weak stomach!

(Mummy Akbar reaches her arm in the air as though waving. Unnoticed by anyone she makes kicking movements in the air, pawing with her feet like pedalling a bicycle and then she lies still. Faruzeh gets up from the bed and crosses the sitting room, ignoring the dining table she walks straight out the door slamming it.)

Mr Akbar: And your daughter?

Old man: Tsk! She must attend to him. *(He nods his head slowly as though meditating the fact.)*

(Fatima looks at Hosro; she winds her ringlet round and round her finger and gives him coy looks from across the table. The dog is seated on his settee next to the old man's chair, devouring the tiny fried meatballs the old man tosses to him. The old man notices Hafsa looking at him sourly.)

Old man: No need to disapprove, not at all! This dog is not a pet but a guard dog. Recently there have been a lot of houses broken into, even in the middle of the night.

186

Mr Akbar: Dogs should be kept outside, even guard dogs.

Old man: How? We live in a flat!

Hafsa: He seems too small for a guard dog, don't you think Uncle?

(Mr Akbar ignores her and keeps on eating.)

Old man: Maybe he is small, but never judge by the size! He also barks every time someone passes by in the hall, now that's useful as a warning isn't it?

Hafsa: I should think it must be very annoying, I expect in a block of flats like this he must be barking on and off all day.

Old man: Well maybe he is, and maybe he isn't.

Mr Akbar: Hafsa, please do not argue this issue. *(He turns to the old man.)* Women need husbands or they start to bicker and think they are equal to a man! Ahh, delicious I must compliment your daughter's cooking!

Old man: A family recipe, my wife, hers were . . . tsk, more clover! Faruzeh now . . . hmm, just so-so. Now, tell me about your plans, I too have been considering opening a new business, maybe some laundry service or this pizza delivery franchise?

(Hosro is staring at his plate ignoring Fatima who's now winding ringlets round her fingers on both sides of her head.)

Fatima: I want to go home!

Mr Akbar: What! What's this?

Fatima: I want to go home and NOW!

Mr Akbar: Nonsense! Shut up. *(He turns back to his plate and carries on eating.)*

Fatima: *(Fatima looks angrily at Hosro.)* He made a rude face at me and he did this *(She holds up her hands, curling her left hand into a tunnel, she feverishly pumps her right index finger in and out the*

187

hole mimicking sexual intercourse. The old man jumps up and lands a heavy clout round Hosro's head. Hamid stands up.)

Hamid: Dad, leave him alone…. I don't believe he did that!

Hosro: *(Wiping his eyes.)* I didn't.

Mr Akbar: *(Stands up.)* Are you calling my daughter a liar?

Hamid: She's just mistaken that's all.

Hafsa: Don't forget Uncle, Fatima and the Kebab boy, she made that up!

Mr Akbar: Shut your mouth! *(Ignoring Hamid, he leans over into Hosro's face.)* Did you or did you not make that disgusting sign to my daughter?

Hosro: *(He jumps up.)* I feel sick! *(He kicks the chair away and stumbles out the room.)*

(The table is silent; Hamid, Mr Akbar and the old man are still standing. Fatima is sitting sulkily with her arms crossed and Hafsa chews down the Baklava faster than a rabbit.)

Mr Akbar: Well I never! *(He kicks back his chair, it falls.)* Fatima, Hafsa, thank Mr Babai for such a wonderful lunch…. We're leaving!

Hafsa: What about Auntie?

(They all turn to look at Mummy Akbar forgotten on the floor, she hasn't moved. Mr Akbar takes a jug of water from the table and goes over to her.)

Mr Akbar: Maimuna? *(He stares down at her, prodding her with his foot.)* MAIMUNA ENOUGH! *(Still she doesn't move but her eyelids flicker. Mr Akbar pours water down on her face from his standing position; it splashes, heavily streaking her face with blotches of make up that run down her cheeks. She now looks like a gargoyle.)*

Hafsa: Uncle, I think you'd better call an ambulance!

188

Mr Akbar: Very well, if I must! *(Unconvinced, he turns to Hamid.)* Where's the telephone?

Hamid: Here. *(He takes the cordless phone from the shelf.)*

Hafsa: *(Giving light little slaps to mummy Akbar.)* Uncle! No need, Auntie has come round.

(Hamid and the old man help her to her feet.)

Mr Akbar: Steady! Steady! That's right! Steady now.

(Mr Akbar leads the way, he opens the door and the old man and Hamid shoulder Mummy Akbar across the sitting room and bump her through the door. Her feet drag and scrabble along the ground, and the two girls follow, exclaiming 'Ooh and Ahh' at each bump. After the old man returns to the sitting room alone and slams the door behind him.)

Old man: *(He looks at the messy dining table.)* Lazy beggars! I'm not clearing up! *(He puts some left over Baklava onto a plate and gives it to the dog.)* Here you are! No need to miss out on the sweets, ehh?

(Then he turns out the light switch and crosses over the darkened sitting room to his bedroom. He takes off his sandals and jacket, and then pulls off his tunic, there are scars criss-crossing his back. He puts on his nightdress and gets into bed, turning out the bedside lamp.)

(The stage darkens quickly to black.)

ACT 1

Scene 10

(The stage lightens slowly to daylight. The old man is lying in bed and Faruzeh is sitting by him on the chair. In the sitting room the muezzin chants are playing on the yellow cassette player. The chandelier is on the floor and Abbas is sweeping up light bulbs into a dustpan. Hosro comes in and out the door clearing the left over dinner things from the table, then Hamid bursts through the door.)

Hamid: What the hell happened?

Abbas: *(Stops sweeping.)* This morning at dawn, the chandelier fell down on top of him while he was praying.

Hamid: *(Shaking head.)* Why the hell did he buy it? I told him it was too heavy for the ceiling, it's a bloody cathedral chandelier!

Abbas: He loved it, it had a thousand watts!

Hamid: What did the Doctor say?

Abbas: *(Shrugs.)* Just concussion, but he's slipping fast from old age, liver failure and kidney failure. He said it would be kinder to let him die at home. His insulin levels are through the roof!

(Hamid walks into the bedroom and sits down on the bed, he pats the bed covers.)

Hamid: *(To Faruzeh.)* How is he?

Faruzeh: He's coming and going. We've called Uncle Aziz, he's on his way here.

Hamid: Why don't you take a break, I'll stay with him. *(Faruzeh ignores him. She stands up and takes a hairbrush from the dressing table and gently brushes*

190

the old man's hair.) Go on, you're still in your nightdress.... Your hair looks worse than his!

Faruzeh: *(She puts the brush down and crosses the sitting room, she stops.)* Abbas, please turn off that bloody muezzin music! And can't you move that chandelier out the way?

Abbas: It's too big to get out the door, it'll have to wait till tomorrow, the toolbox is at the shop.

Faruzeh: I'm going to have a shower, can you sort the kitchen? *(Abbas sets his broom against the table and turns off the muezzin tape. He and Hosro follow Faruzeh out the sitting room door.)*

Hamid: *(Hamid is still sitting on the bed and is gently shaking the old man's shoulder.)* Dad, can you hear me? *(The old man's eyes open, he lifts his head up off the pillow.)* Dad, you're awake! Say something. Dad?

Old man: Help me sit up. *(Hamid pulls him forwards and plumps up the pillows behind his head, then lets him back down.)* Ouch! Be more careful.

Hamid: Dad, you've come round, you're going to be all right!

Old man: All right my arse! I heard the doctor, I'm done for, I'm like an old banger, not worth repairing, nothing to be done! *(Doorbell rings.)* Don't let that fool Aziz come in here! I don't want him.

Hamid: Dad? How can you say that when he's your own brother?

Old man: Don't care!

(Abbas leads Uncle Aziz through the sitting room door. He's a tall thin man wearing a dark tunic and a fez hat. He is carrying a leather bound Quran.)

Abbas: Thank you for coming. *(They kiss on each cheek.)* We thought you'd be hungry so we're

191

preparing some food, I'll call you when it's ready. *(Abbas points to the old man's room.)* He's through there. *(Uncle Aziz walks into the bedroom and Abbas begins to lay the dining table, taking glasses and plates from the shelf unit.)*

Uncle Aziz: Brother I have come. *(He sits down on the chair and turns to Hamid.)* Go and fetch another chair, it's not right to sit upon the bed of a dying man!

Old man: I want him on the bed and I want Cyrus too.

Uncle Aziz: Who is this Cyrus?

Old man: Never you mind, keep your nose out my business, I'm perfectly well, just a false alarm. I'm not dying so you can go and stuff your face along with my donkey son-in-law and then go back to where you came from.

Uncle Aziz: Bitter as ever! Not even in the jaws of death can you hold your tongue. You even begrudge me a little rice!

Old man: Bitter! And why not? Here I am dying, has anyone asked me if I'm hungry? No they haven't! Even a condemned murderer gets his last supper, anything he wants, and they even have caviar and champagne on death row in America!

Uncle Aziz: You'll not swerve me from my duty, I have come here to recite the Surah thirty-six and I shall whisper the Shahadah as is prescribed. *(He opens the Quran, flicks through the pages and begins reciting in a whisper.)*

Old man: *(To Hamid.)* Go and fetch Cyrus, it's my only hope....

(Hamid goes through the sitting room, out the door, and returns carrying the dog into the bedroom. He puts him on the bed.)

Uncle Aziz: What is this abomination? How dare you! *(Looking at Hamid.)* Take this filthy dog from my sight or I will leave this cursed home right now!

Old man: Hamid sit down on the bed too! Your uncle Aziz is going! *(Uncle Aziz slams the Quran shut and stands up shaking his head in disbelief. Abbas can hear them quarrelling. He stops laying the table and stands just outside the bedroom doorway peering in.)*

Uncle Aziz: *(Jabbing his finger at Hamid.)* You have failed your father! You fail in your duties as a son! You are pandering to the whims of a senile confused old man. *(Points to the old man.)* And you are condemning yourself to the lowest pit of hell! Hypocrisy is the most dangerous sin. You claim to believe! Yet you denounce your faith and all that is good with this filthy dog's presence. You'll go to Hawiyah!

Old man: Get out!

(Uncle Aziz stands up and storms out nearly colliding with Abbas in the doorway. He strides through the sitting room and out the door. Abbas enters the old man's bedroom quietly.)

Hamid: Dad what's going on?

Old man: A thousand watt chandelier fell on my head, what do you expect? I don't want bloody prayers, I want a drink! Ahh! I remember the taste, whisky, I used to drink whisky, and you didn't know that did you? It's the one thing I want now!

Abbas: Maybe he's delirious....

Hamid: Maybe he isn't! Look go and fetch that bottle we keep under the kitchen sink. *(Abbas leaves and goes out the sitting room door.)* I never knew you drank Dad. *(Looking at the old man shaking his head in wonderment.)*

Old man: I didn't want you to know I was a bad man!
All these years I have believed it, but you know
what? *(He grasps Hamid by his shirt, clinging on.)*
Maybe I'm not so bad? Maybe we're not bad! *(He
falls back on the pillows, letting go of Hamid.)*
You've never been a bad son, just a fool. We're all
fools! And do you know Hamid? I think it's a good
thing to be! *(He grips hold of Hamid's shirt pulling
himself up.)* Can you believe I committed adultery?
(Hamid shakes his head.) Well I did, for seven
weeks! I met a beautiful girl each morning under a
mulberry tree. I remember the mulberries still cool
from the night air, shaken from an old tree heavy
with deep red mulberries. She and I stood together
watching them fall. We could just taste each
mulberry as they fell on the snow-white shawl I'd
lain at the foot of the gnarled tree trunk. We
devoured cool sweet juicy mulberries under an
orange sky as the sun rose, our mouths smeared red
as we lay by a silver stream on a white shawl stained
red, and the wind stirred the leaves as they rustled
and gently fluttered in the breeze. Was it wrong?
How can it be wrong? *(He lets go of Hamid and falls
back on the pillows.)*

Hamid: It wasn't wrong Dad....

Old man: *(He smiles.)* It was the most wondrous thing.
Something that wonderful can never be wrong! It
all happened during the revolution, but we were
found out and punished . . . Khomeini was in power
by then. I was flogged.... *(He clutches Hamid's
shoulder.)* But worse! A few weeks later some men
threw acid in her face, it was all burnt away! She had
no lips anymore, lips that were once sweet and red.
(He traces Hamid's lips.) Just think Hamid! Can you
picture that? *(He sits up again holding on to Hamid's*

194

shirt.) Your mother was shamed, everyone knew, that's the real reason why we had to leave. You see this girl lived on the same street as us, after it happened, after her face was ruined I couldn't stay. Was I bad? Was it my fault?

Hamid: No Dad, it was never your fault, shit just happens....

Old man: You see I never really loved your mother, I didn't choose her, she didn't choose me. If I had the chance I'd lie under the mulberry tree with that beautiful girl again and again, I don't care how high the price is! Why does there have to be a price? Don't you see? *(He grips Hamid's shirt closer to him.)* It was their fault! They made us pay! All these years I've been sick with guilt . . . but I'm not guilty am I?

Hamid: You were never guilty Dad!

Old man: I know, it was them! They did it, they make the crime and they make the punishment. I want to live in a free world where you don't have to pay. *(He falls back on the pillows.)* And that's the truth and now you know!

Hamid: You told us the scars on your back were from the war.

Old man: They are war scars, just a different war.

(Abbas, Faruzeh and Hosro come into the bedroom. Abbas has a bottle of whisky and a glass.)

Hamid: Dad, look Abbas has brought you the whisky, do you still want some?

Old man: Of course! And fill the glass, fill it to the brim, let it overflow, it will be my last. *(Abbas fills the glass to overflowing and passes it to Hamid who gently holds it to the old man's lips. He lifts his head and drinks it down greedily like a baby sucking milk from a teat. He drains it all and falls back on his*

195

pillows. Slowly Abbas, Faruzeh and Hosro gather together on the other side of the bed.) Ahh! That feels so good! I always thought I could beat the evil out of me, but it never worked, look at me now. Ha ha! *(He coughs.)*

Hamid: You were never evil Dad. *(He takes the old man's hand.)*

Old man: *(He pulls himself up, eyes wide open.)* But will I go to heaven or hell?

Hamid: Heaven!

Faruzeh: Heaven.

Abbas: You'll go to heaven.

Hosro: Of course you'll go to heaven Baba!

Old man: *(He sinks back down on the pillows. He sighs deeply.)* Tell me about heaven, what will heaven be like? Is it true what they say?

Abbas: There will be rivers of wine that will be delicious to those that drink.

Hosro: Bunches of fruit will hang low within your reach. Vessels of silver and cups of crystal will be passed around.

Faruzeh: You will be served by young boys as handsome as pearls. You will wear the finest silk clothing and sit upon a throne made of gold and decorated with precious stones.

Old man: And the Virgin Angels? The Houris?

Hamid: Heaven is full of them!

Old man: Just tell me about the Houris. *(He shuts his eyes, smiling.)*

Hamid: In the gardens of heaven will be virgins of modest gaze, reclining on couches of happiness arranged in rows, their faces as bright as the shining stars in heaven. Like red wine in a white glass, with large, round, pointed breasts that are high and never dangle. They never pee nor poo, they have no hairy

196

legs and armpits just long luxurious hair and eyebrows like swallows wings. They never sweat nor smell bad, and they never menstruate or bear children. A Houri does not want your wife to annoy you during your life on earth, as the Houri will be your wife when you go to heaven.

Old man: I think I'm going, I can feel it! . . . Wait! *(He opens his eyes lifting his head and points at Abbas who is crying and wiping his eyes with his sleeves.)* You bugger off! I don't want you going Hee Haw like a bloody donkey! Tsk! *(Abbas stumbles round the bed and out the room. He sits down on the sofa in the sitting room and blows his nose.)* Hosro?

Hosro: Yes Baba?

Old man: Look after Cyrus, promise me you'll take care of him. I have been looking into the numerology and it is no coincidence that God is Dog backwards! *(He lies back down.)* Now silence! I will begin my ascent to heaven.

(Lights darken slowly to black, curtain down.)

The small man builds cages for everyone he knows.
While the sage,
who has to duck his head when the moon is low,
keeps dropping keys all night long
for the beautiful rowdy prisoners.

Hafiz

Lightning Source UK Ltd.
Milton Keynes UK
UKOW041009311012

201461UK00001B/8/P